OUT OF THE PITCH

By Dave Semple

Dave Semple

This book is a work of fiction. Names, characters, places and incidents either are the product of the author's imagination or are used fictitiously. Any resemblance to actual persons, living or dead, events, or locales is entirely coincidental.

© 2017 by Dave Semple

All rights reserved. Copyright under Berne Copyright Convention, Universal Copyright Convention, and Pan-American Copyright Convention. No part of this book may be reproduced, stored in a retrieval system, or transmitted in any form, or by any means, electronic, mechanical, photocopying, recording or otherwise, without prior permission of the author.

ISBN-13:
978-1547297344

ISBN-10:
1547297344

First Edition

Always for Susan
who keeps believing in me
even when I don't.

For my bigs and my not-so-wees
who keep inspiring me to improve.

The truth is just a lie that hasn't been found out.
- Robert Ludlum -

1

From a church balcony on Christmas Eve... gradually, a memory emerges... a minister, wearing a robe adorned with a festively embroidered stole, moves slowly from the pulpit below me towards the congregation, a shoe box in each extended hand. She removes the lid from the first box... the darkness released from within has no effect on its surroundings. Light fades to nothing... now the sanctuary is in total darkness. As she slowly lifts the lid from the second box the gleam from a hidden flashlight effuses, highlighting her face like a figure in the dramatic illumination and shadows of a Caravaggio masterpiece. A tenebrism from long ago, from far away. I don't remember the sermon or the carols, but I do remember the image: two boxes, the darkness, the light bursting forth.

What I wouldn't give right now for that second box. I've lost track of how long I've been wrapped in the darkness of this cell. I'm not sure I'll ever see light again. I'm not even sure I want to, knowing what I now know.

You open your eyes. There is nothing. There is no difference between your eyes being open and your eyes being closed. There is only blackness. Even at night, you have always seen something, some ambient piece of something shining, glowing, illuminating. There was a difference between eyes open and eyes closed. Not here. Not now.

Here, there is nothing. Truly nothing.

You are on the floor. It's hard. Concrete. The weight of your hands feels its roughness. You can feel your hands, but you can't move them. You try. Nothing. Not even a finger. The signals from your mind are not making the connection. There is sensation sending signals brainward, but there is no response. Same with your legs.

You are looking up, lying on your back. At least your other senses tell you that you're on your back. The canals in your inner ears say you are lying on your back looking up. But you can only be looking up if you can see something. There is nothing. Not nothing. Something. Darkness. Darkness is something. Your body won't move. Again, you try. Caught between asleep and awake. Your brain is screaming to your limbs to move but they are deaf and you are blind.

Perhaps it isn't darkness. Is it blindness? Have you gone blind?

Searing ache. Everything burns. Paralyzed. Are you paralyzed? Paralysis would explain the non-conformity of your limbs. Has something happened, leaving you both blind and paralyzed?

If you are paralyzed, you will not be able to feel the texture beneath your hands and the coldness, but the floor is damp and clammy. You can feel it with your heels as well. Your feet are bare. There are clothes, though. You aren't naked. You can feel the rough fabric on your skin. Paralysis ruled out.

You are breathing. The movement is shallow, but there. Mouth breathing. Your tongue is dry, desert dry. Cracking dry. It won't move to the roof. It is just lying in the bottom of your mouth.

You blink. You think you blink. Slow blink. You're not sure. There is no difference between open and closed. There is only a sensation of movement.

Everything is foggy, mountain-valley-in-the-cool-morning foggy. You want the fog to lift, but it lingers - a cold, wet blanket upon you, full-body water-boarding. The weight upon your chest grows. The breaths, more shallow, more frequent. Panic. Can't breathe. Hyperventilation.

Unconsciousness.

3

Daylight-savings dusk. The air was wet as the day's unusual spring heat slipped away in waves. He rode his bicycle home from work through the park, transitioning from city to suburbs on the meandering bike paths divided by yellow lines and directional arrows designed to minimize chaos.

He passed by the dog walkers, the joggers, the after-dinner parents pushing strollers, the kids on their skateboards and long-boards and BMX bikes as they postponed their sundown curfews.

"On your left." *Ding, ding* from the rear.

"Really? I'm as far right as I can be without riding on the grass," he thought. "Damn cyclenazis." Mr. 'Buff and Lean' breezed by on his red and black Pinarello, clad in his red and black lycra riding shorts and shirt and matching streamlined teardrop helmet. "Poser. Bet he'll be posting his ride with a selfie for everyone to see. Why can't people just grow up and slow down?"

He caught himself sounding like a grumpy octogenarian even though he wasn't halfway there yet. He didn't care. He'd always been mature for his age, ahead of the curve, cutting-edge. People just didn't appreciate his forward thinking nature. "Hope he gets hit at an intersection."

This evening's class had been uneventful, but then again, his mind had been elsewhere. Twenty-three wanna-be writers sitting in a circle sharing their drivel and telling each other how insightful and creative they were. He would step in and point out their clichés, their predictability, their terrible metaphors, their superficial characterizations.

He reveled in the knowledge that they referred to him as "Kill-joy" behind his back. It was his job, after all. He wasn't going to molly-coddle their fragile self-esteems as their high school teachers had. If they really wanted to be writers, they had to get used to being beaten up on a daily basis. Writing was not for the weak. If they survived his first-year introduction to creative writing course, those with potential might and actually sign up for second year. He was just separating the wheat from the chaff.

Whenever one of the students challenged his criticisms, he smiled dryly and said, "And during the day, I work as lead editor at a major publishing house. You are absolutely correct. I have no idea what I am talking about." Five years ago he had started teaching at the college to pay for the in-ground pool. He continued to teach the course to protect the world from bad writing. The job also kept him out of the house.

Two nights a week, from seven to eight-thirty, he held court over their creative little mostly freshman souls. He lived to pounce and claw his way through their whining prose and self-indulgent poetry. Most of their efforts actually caused him physical pain, usually a constriction of the lower intestines and sphincter. When the discomfort migrated into his scrotum, he lashed out.

"Well, that was shit. How many times do we have to hear about the angst of unrequited love? Find a new angle."

"And what nocturnal emission inspired you to commit this to paper?" he once said, waving the submission through the air. "Or was this what you used to clean up the mess?"

"The most engaging part of your story was the period at the end."

His brutal remarks gave him great joy. Each session left him invigorated, aroused. Not literally, but near enough. These reactions were the closest thing to sexual passion in his life lately.

As much as he enjoyed tearing their work apart, he was looking forward to the end of the semester and the coming summer. This batch of scribblers was becoming tedious and whiny as the reality of their grade point averages was not living up to their parents' standards. There wasn't a spark of originality among them. In most groups there had been at least one or two in whom he could see some progress, some hope of genuine thought and creativity; but these individuals were dull elementary school pencils.

No, the end of semester could not come soon enough - especially after the meeting he had endured with the department head before class.

4

Cold. So cold your muscles are on fire. Every joint is aching. You can't feel your fingers or your toes and you can hear machine-gun fire. It's echoing inside your skull. *Rata-tat-a-rata-tat*. The noise won't stop. Neither will the throbbing in your temples. *Rata-tat-a-rata-tat*. It's not machine-gun fire. It's your teeth. You are shivering.

You open your eyes. Nothing but darkness. Eyes open, eyes closed, there's no difference.

This time, you can move. You draw your arms up over your chest as the shivering verges on convulsion. You remember reading somewhere to stick your freezing hands under your armpits. Your fingers cramp as the pressure from your biceps bears down on them against your ribs. You roll over onto your side and pull your knees up to try to conserve a modicum of warmth. You are a shuddering fetal ball on the rough concrete. Every shiver scrapes your skin. Your head spasms against the floor as the cells vibrate in the attempt to create heat.

In the darkness you sit up. You know you have to move. You have to get the blood circulating through your body or you're going to freeze to death. You try to stand. No strength in your legs. You fall. The concrete claws your skin and rips at your numb hands as they catch your weight, like landing on jagged ice in February. Again, you try. Your head hits the ceiling when you are halfway up. Down to the floor. You hit hard. Your hands fly up to your head to hold it together. Your ears ring and you feel nauseous. Your neck twinges as the impact knocks vertebra out of alignment.

You try once more, this time hunched over to lower your centre of gravity and to avoid a concussion. You will whatever strength you have in your body into your legs. Your hands reach up to determine the ceiling. You make it to your knees. You cannot see anything. You have no idea where you are. You are tentative as you reach out in your blindness but you grasp only air.

"Hello," you rasp into the obscurity. The sound comes back quickly, your own voice. The space is small, claustrophobic. "Hello," stronger this time. Your voice only confirms the closeness of the walls.

You take a kneeling step and reach out again, above and to the side. Nothing. Another kneeling step and your fingers find a wall. More concrete. Rough, like the floor. You fumble to your left in search of a door. One step. Two steps. Only a wall. A few more cautious steps and the wall briefly turns away.

The door. Not very tall. Four feet, tops. Metal. The enamel paint is chipped. Your fingertips feel the uneven edges. Not chipped. Scratched. Clawed. There is no window, just a solid metal door, sealed at the edges. Rubber. There are no handles or hinges . The door must swing out toward freedom. You pound your fists on the metal as you yell, "Let me out!" over and over. Your voice is dry and raw and begins to give out. Your hands ache, but at least the metal doesn't rip your skin. You stop to listen, hoping for footsteps or a voice from beyond.

Nothing. Silence. The sound of your own laboured breathing bouncing back, metallic, as your forehead resigns itself to the barrier.

Above the door, the wall arches toward you, becoming a ceiling, curving in. With one foot under, you rise slowly from your knees, delicately tracing the flow from wall to ceiling as it moves away from the door. You are crouched, and the effort burns your thighs. The ceiling continues to curve upward, away from the door, as your fingers continue their course.

Suddenly, your right foot steps into emptiness, a hole in the floor. Your leg is swallowed to the thigh, torqueing your hip. You catch yourself before the femur snaps and you land hard on your left knee. The muscles in your groin stretch beyond their limit and you think you feel something tear. You catch your breath and extricate your leg. The scrapes bite. Your groin burns.

You crawl back toward the door, but it's not where you left it. Everything is turned around in the black. You are disoriented. Everything is spinning. You hug the floor, the only real constant, and make your way back to the wall, then feel your way, again, to the door. The exertion has brought you some warmth, but still you shiver. You draw yourself up, huddling on the floor, your shoulder moulding itself into the jamb.

"Why the hell am I here?" you call out, your voice quavering. "What do you want with me? I'm nobody."

Your hand falls to the side. It lands on something soft. Not soft, just softer than the concrete. Rough surface. Wool. A blanket. A folded woolen blanket.

5

The mind works in mysterious ways. Moments long forgotten can rise to the surface and burst through the ice of the present, triggered by the most insignificant experience: a song, a smell, a taste, a touch, a mood. Some of them struggle upwards from the darkness of great depths. Then one image of frozen time bumps into others; they begin to toppling one by one like dominoes until they rest upon each other in jagged layers.

    Gradually a brush of memory on the gessoed canvas of my mind reveals a scene. I fell through the ice when I was young while on a winter ice-fishing trip with a friend and his father. No one caught anything, and boredom led to inattentiveness, until I stepped into one of the augered holes, all the way to my thigh. When the black water surged upwards through the opening I instantly found myself sitting in a pool of freezing cold. The panicked father rushed over to release me from my trap. The boot didn't survive, lost to the frigid lake. Soaked from the waist down in an air temperature of minus twenty, I became terrified as approaching hypothermia ripped the heat from my numbing legs.

We raced forever on two snowmobiles over the white contours of the frameless landscape until we finally arrived at the big blue Cadillac that had brought us on this expedition. The father rapidly pulled a blanket from the trunk, wrapping me in its rough grey wool. That blanket was my savior.

6

There had been a message in his inbox summoning him to her office. He thought it odd that she wanted to meet before class. She wasn't known to stay past four and he didn't usually arrive at the campus until six, after finishing up at the publishing house and grabbing a bite to eat on the way.

His philosophy regarding administrators was: the less contact, the better. Never give them much time to talk or they'll prattle on ad infinitum.

He knocked on her door at six-forty.

"What can I help you with?" he asked as he took a seat in front of her desk.

"One of your students was admitted to hospital this morning. Suicide attempt. His roommate tried to wake him for class but couldn't and called an ambulance."

"Which one?"

"Jarrod Turning. He's in stable condition now, after they got the pills out of his system."

"Well, thank you for letting me know. I haven't seen him in a couple of weeks. I just thought he'd dropped the course to focus his efforts on other classes, those he stood a chance of passing."

She sat back in her chair. "I'm aware the two of you were not getting along very well."

"Getting along?"

"You have been very critical of his work in your course…"

"No more than I've been with anyone else."

"Not according to his mother. She contacted me this afternoon once Jarrod had regained consciousness."

"His mother? What does she have to do with anything?"

"She says you have been belittling and demeaning him in front of his peers with everything he has written for your course."

"He's a terrible writer. He keeps submitting trite poetry about the girlfriend who obviously dumped him during the Christmas break."

"So, you know he's been going through some difficulties?"

"Difficulties? They're all going through difficulties. It's called life." He could feel his blood pressure rising. "This Jarrod, he's what, in his twenties? His final year if I remember correctly. And English isn't even his major. At the beginning of the course he said he thought intro creative writing would be a bird and he needed one more arts credit. As for his mother, if he's calling her every day to whimper about his life, it's no wonder the girlfriend dumped him. The mother is just looking for someone to blame…"

"Enough," she said, cutting him off. "There are certainly other contributing factors at play in this young man's life. I'm just pointing out that the way in which you offer criticism to your students may be more critical than it is constructive, and this may be one of the issues in this particular instance."

"What am I supposed to do? Tell them it's all sunshine

and roses? Have them all believe they are destined to become the defining voices of the future? They're not, not that I've seen anyway." He took a moment. "You hired me to teach them how to be better writers. It takes criticism. I am not their friend. I am not their therapist. I don't care if they want to exorcize their demons through their writing, all power to them, it's what writers do, but at least make the effort to write well and to improve. If they need emotional help, there are on-campus services, if I'm not wrong. Hell, aren't we even bringing in therapy dogs at midterms and finals for them to pet to alleviate their anxieties and soothe their tortured souls? To succeed, the unmotivated just need a good swift kick in the ass."

"Are you done?" She was not impressed. They stared at each other for a moment across the oak desk. She was waiting for an apology or some act of contrition for his outburst. He gave her none.

"You were hired," she began in a firm but collected tone, "to inspire those with an interest in writing to explore their talents, to make improvements and become better at the craft, but more importantly, to provide a safe place for growth to happen..."

"A safe place? Please..."

"I'm not done." She waited for him to show some resignation. With a deep breath, he gave it. She continued, "Young people require encouragement. It has to balance the criticism. It's how this all works. When I hired you for the position, I will confess, your association with Smyth Publishing was a selling point. It is important for our institution to make in-roads with the professional community, and some of our graduating students have found employment and established valuable internships, but that network has been firmly forged, with your assistance, of course." She let her remarks settle in for a moment.

"Now I need you to be a more positive force in their education. Encouragement is an area in which you are lacking. I've gone through the course evaluations filled out by your students over the last couple of years. Yes, there are a few who have loved how challenging your instruction has been, but the majority finds you to be, quite frankly, a bully. If you wish to continue your association with this department and this institution next year, you might want to consider this constructive criticism I'm offering you and implement it between now and finals. Please do - how did you put it - at least try to make the effort to improve."

She had drawn her line in the sand.

"I've read those evaluations, too," he said, rising from his seat. "I find them to be quite entertaining. Now, I have a class to teach and I wouldn't want to be late. I'll take what you've said under advisement, but if you're going to hold a gun to my head, make sure you pull the trigger," and he left.

I learned to fragment my mind early on. Creating separate selves was neither a choice nor a conscious decision. It just happened when, in my despair, I no longer recognized my own voice. Survival by disassociation.

I'm not in a cell. This is happening to a character I have created so that I can survive this ordeal. When I picture your hours in the darkness and solitude I know that I could not possibly endure those soul-threatening conditions, so this tale cannot always be mine. Sometimes it will have to be *yours*. And the memories that etch themselves upon your mind might become *his* story.

To pass the time, and to preserve our sanities, we will sketch the penciled outlines of our previous lives and pastel the details in delicate hues. The trio of dissembling creators shall thereby prepare a triptych of multilayered scenes of shimmering reflections.

8

He had a teacher in high school, a pig of a man who wore dirty old pants, worn leather shoes, and pit-stained button-shirts. No wonder this guy was single. He taught science from the throne behind his desk. He'd scribble notes on the blackboard, then sprawl in his chair and, from his cluttered pulpit, try to proselytize us to his superior understanding of the world, while swirling messy hair with his fingers. Science and math were his religion, and anything beyond he deemed frivolous.

His family lived in a lumber town up north. The school was small. The community was working-class. Everyone had a relative who worked in the bush or at the mill, or hauled lumber south. Most of the kids his age were destined for the same life and they knew it. They even accepted it.

Not him. He wanted the hell out. He made the mistake one day of answering this teacher's question honestly.

"So, what 'cha plan to do when you graduate?" the teacher asked while the class wrote down the day's notes.

"University for Journalism," he replied without thinking.

"What are ya? Some kinda artsy fartsy faggot?"

His classmates didn't even try to stifle their laughter. He'd always been an outsider in their world of hunting, fishing, and hockey.

He wanted so badly to talk back, to say what an ignorant prick the son-of-a-bitch was, but his terror of the man froze his vocal chords. This was the person, in a position of authority, who had left an imprint of Jimmy Hargraves' head and shoulders in the locker outside his classroom the year before when Jimmy, a dumb brute of a kid, had asked, "Could you stop rambling on because it's putting me to sleep?" No challenge went unpunished.

Finally he muttered, "I like to write."

"Well, good luck with that," prompting more laughter from the class. "You're never gonna make it, you know. You don't have what it takes. My bets are you'll drop out and be back here workin' at the mill within two years."

He could only stare, teeth clenched, ears burning with rage and humiliation. But he didn't run home to tell his mother and father. They always had their hands full anyway. Besides, he'd been dealing with the Neanderthals at school for years. This was just an adult version. No, he did what he'd taught himself to do: put it all into a box and bury it deep inside. It's what everyone else seemed to do, except for his younger brother. If anyone was the artsy fartsy faggot, he was. He didn't really believe that, he just knew it was a mean thing to think about his brother.

When university began in the fall he could still hear the words, "You're never gonna make it," echoing from inside the box. The voice was both a seed of doubt and a call to battle. For the next four years, anytime he experienced failure he would pull out the box and crack open its lid, reliving the memory of that day. No matter what, he was going to prove the son-of-a-bitch wrong.

Each time he re-examined that moment, he wrote a fiction of the future in his head, adding to it with every setback. In this story, he would go home after graduation with a diploma in one hand and a job offer in the other. He would return to the school and confront the son-of-a-bitch. He would walk into the classroom, toss his diploma on the desk and tell him to go fuck himself.

This delicious machination sustained him during the challenging years of university, and as the end of undergrad arrived, he could taste the possibility of this fiction becoming a reality.

There were no job offers, but the diploma was in hand: a major in English Literature and a minor in Art History. He headed home after convocation in May for a short visit.

His family had driven down for the ceremony and he decided to take a week off from his part-time jobs to return with them before seriously trying to hunt down employment that made use of the new degree.

On Friday night the family arrived home. On Monday he would go to the school and fulfill his destiny.

9

You cocoon yourself in the blanket and huddle in the doorframe trying your best to preserve as much heat as possible. You rock back and forth, your teeth still beating a tattoo inside your head. You're not sure how long you've been here. You can't remember. You bring your hand to your face. Stubble. It feels like two or three days' growth. Your beard is your only way of judging time. If it has been three days, that's how long you haven't eaten. Hunger and thirst settle in. Your stomach is tight and cramped, but you attribute your discomfort to the cold.

The back of your head screams. There is such pressure it could erupt at any moment. You can't lean it on the door without electric waves bolting through to your eye sockets.

That's how they must have subdued you. Whoever has you must have struck you across the back of your head with a pipe or a bat.

The questions in your head become your words. "Where am I? Why am I here? What have I done? What are you doing to me?" interwoven with sobs you fight, in vain, to hold back.

You try to think back to the last thing you remember

before waking up in the darkness. It's all too hazy. You went to work in the morning. You rode your bike. You had lunch in the deli across the street. There was a meeting with the other editors but you can't remember the details. No. That meeting was a week ago. It's all jumbled. You watched your daughter's soccer game. Which night? She almost scored, caught the post instead. Thursday? What day is it now? It's too much. You can't hold on to your own thoughts. The strain makes you want to vomit. You swallow down hard. Keep it in. Maybe if you lie on your side. You ease yourself down, your cheek to the floor. It's cold. It's soothing.

You can't figure out why it's soothing because you're freezing, so cold your body still shudders. You realize you're sweating. Sweating? How can it be? Fever. You're not cold. You're burning up!

Lying down does not help your stomach. The bile creeps up your esophagus. It's burning. You can't hold it back so you stop fighting and out it comes, the acid scorching your throat. Another wave, then another, your stomach wrings itself out and the effort increases the pounding in your head. You roll away from the mess and the stench. The darkness spins faster. You are in a centrifuge. Your eyelids squeeze tight to try to hold everything in. Just when your cells are about to explode, you disappear.

10

My parents took us to Yellowstone one summer. I think I was eleven or twelve because my baby brother had just figured out how to walk and was more than a handful in his newfound mobility. Because he had been named after my father, everyone just called him Junior. We spent two days driving through the park, seeing the sights, and going on long hikes. I hated it. Nature and I never got along very well.

On the third day we went to some caves outside the park, the Lewis and Clark Caverns. The name hints of Lewis and Clark having discovered them. They didn't. It was a marketing ploy to honour the great explorers and cartographers who did, indeed, map the Jefferson River nearby, but they never even knew of the caverns' existence. "Lewis and Clark" had a better ring to it than "Brooke and Mexican John" or "Williams and Pannell". I learned this information from our guide. It's funny what details stick with you over time.

This guide was awesome. He was a college graduate who had no plans for using his worthless degree; however, he'd been working at the caverns for the past few summers and he was continuing to avoid reality for one more tourist season.

I loved his sarcastic tone as he delivered the relevant historical and geographical information interspersed with lame jokes I remember finding hilarious, but which made the adults groan. The caverns were astounding to my pre-teen eyes. I asked lots of questions and I loved how the guide answered them.

After we had arrived at one of the lowest rooms, cordoned off from a ledge, he turned off all the lights, plunging our group into utter darkness. We all stood in silence as the blanket of black overtook us. He proceeded to tell us a tale. "One particular gentleman didn't want to pay Williams the price of admission to see the caves so he decided to come down here on his own. Now, remember, the only light they had back then came from candles. A candle lasted about five hours if you were lucky. Also keep in mind these lovely stairs you've been descending hadn't been built yet, so people explored the caves by lowering themselves down on a rope... while holding a candle. Oh, and the women did it in full-length skirts and petticoats. Most intelligent people would bring more than one candle, but not this genius. He figured he'd be in and out in a flash. All he had with him was a canteen of water. Anyway, he'd managed to get to this point in the caves through sheer ignorance. His rope wasn't quite long enough, about ten feet shy of the ground in this particular cavern. So, what did he decide to do?" The guide paused for effect. "Go back up the rope like anyone with half a brain would have done? Nope. He decided to drop the last ten feet while holding his ever-shortening candle in his mouth."

We all laughed as the image formed in our minds.

"As his feet hit the ground, his teeth clamped together, then popped apart. The candle went flying, falling farther down the chasm, extinguishing as it fell. There he was, in the dark like y'all are now. His candle was gone and he couldn't reach the rope. Hell, he couldn't even see where it was to reach for it.

What are ya gonna do?" No one had an answer because there wasn't one.

"Is anyone here feeling a little dizzy?" he continued. His question was answered by affirmative mumbles from many on the tour. The sensation was real. I was off-balance and my stomach felt a bit weird.

"That's vertigo. Once you take away the sense of sight, many people lose their ability to maintain their equilibrium and they become disoriented." He clicked the lights back on, much to everyone's relief.

"He was down here for five days before Williams brought another tour through. He had no idea where he was, but he was hugging a stalagmite for dear life just to keep grounded and he was babbling incoherently like a baby. And that, my friends, is why Darwinism is so important to humanity."

During my first few weeks here I felt the same as the incautious tourist, clinging to the floor, unsure of which direction was up or down, left or right. I still babble to myself from time to time, but when I catch myself, I try to focus on a memory in the hopes of holding myself together, seeking a glimmer of light in my darkness. That's what I just did, about the Lewis and Clark Caverns. It's the only way I've lasted this long, one memory at a time.

Didn't the guy have matches with him to light the candle before he began his descent? It's a detail that has always bothered me. There are details that detract from a story. Embellishment and omission: tools of the trade, in writing and in life.

11

He had a difficult time falling asleep the night before, tossing and turning in excitement and anticipation of the confrontation ahead. He played it all out in his mind: walking into the classroom, diploma in hand; picturing the son-of-a-bitch spread out in his chair behind his desk, his nostrils flaring like the pig he was; tossing the diploma perfectly onto the desk atop the clutter; looking the teacher squarely in the eye and savouring each syllable as it dripped from his mouth, "Fuck. You." He wished there were more syllables to savour. The scenario gave him chills, just thinking about it. He had even laid out his wardrobe before going to bed. He ate a big breakfast Monday morning after sleeping in. His mother's pancakes had never tasted so good. Impending retribution makes everything taste better.

The trek to his alma mater was refreshing. Magnolias were in bloom. Birds were singing. The sun was shining. He arrived as planned, just as the students were exiting the building for lunch. Slipping in the side door, he climbed the stairs to the second floor. He wanted to avoid meeting anyone who would distract him from his mission, other teachers who might want to say hello.

    The stomach butterflies, which started on the landing before the last flight, fluttered more vigorously with each step. When he reached the top of the stairs he thought he might chicken out. Jimmy's imprint remained in the locker. He stopped for a moment to gather his wits. This was the moment. He took a deep breath and stepped across the threshold into the classroom.

    The son-of-a-bitch wasn't there. The classroom was empty. "Shit," he muttered.

12

Two thousand four hundred and fifty-four days. That is how long Terry Anderson, the journalist, spent in captivity from 1985 to 1991. His second daughter was born three months after he had been taken hostage by Shiite Hezbollah militants, backed by Iran, in an attempt to compel US forces to withdraw from Lebanon. He lost a brother and a father while in captivity.

I was thirteen years old when he was released. My parents had followed the story in the papers, on the radio, and on the nightly television news. I wonder if he was part of the reason I wanted to explore journalism. Maybe I'm just projecting.

I remember seeing a photograph in the newspaper upon Terry's release of him and his daughter, together for the first time. She was six years old and wore a red coat. She was holding her father's hand.

Of all of his time in captivity, he spent just over a year in solitary confinement, blindfolded and chained. When interviewers asked how he endured his isolation, he replied that he had relived moments from his life in his mind to keep from going insane. "You do what you have to do, hopefully with a little grace and dignity."

Terry Anderson has become my role model in my own confinement. I wonder if he had to create other personae as I have had to divide my psyche into a triad of souls. If I am going to get through this trial, I will do whatever I must do, hopefully with a little grace and dignity.

13

"Professor?"

He snapped from his reverie. "Yes?"

"Have you any suggestions for me?" she asked tentatively.

The commentary from the other students in the circle had come to an end and, as was customary, they expected him to have the last word.

"I have nothing to add. I think it's about as good as it's going to get." He didn't want them know that he hadn't been paying attention.

"So," she began, a hopefulness brushing across her face, "you think it's good? The way it is?"

"I didn't say that. I definitely did not say that."

She melted into her chair.

The meeting with his supervisor had irked him more than he was willing to admit. He knew what he was doing. He was justified in his methods. Yes, there had been a brief moment as he left her office when he considered the possibility that she might have been right, but he quickly pushed the thought aside and chose to play politics.

Synchronicity had provided him with an ally on the Board of Directors. A recent addition, she held sway because of her recent rise in celebrity for her latest novel, published by Smyth Publishing and edited by none other than himself.

There was no denying that she was a stellar writer. But they both knew that his last, fresh eyes on her work were what made it pop. She had sung the editor's praises in the acknowledgements of her last three books, one of which was being made into a movie. Sure, she was wingy and self-absorbed, but they were on the same page when it came to the future of writing as an art form. "It's all crap. They let them get away with writing superficial crap and the world just laps it up," she'd often say after a few drinks.

He had called her during his walk across campus to let her know the details of his meeting and of the threat levelled against him. He was certain she would have his back if he was threatened with dismissal. His message had gone to voicemail.

Now he was looking at his phone. No messages. The students let him know, with the rustle of pens, papers, and laptops being stuffed into backpacks, that it was time to wrap things up.

"Ladies and gentlemen, our passage through space has come to an end for another week. I will remind you that your final projects are due two weeks from tonight. Now, out with you."

He walked back to his closet of an office, grabbed his helmet, hurried from the building, unlocked his bike from the rack, and headed home.

14

You wake up. Maybe not wake up. You regain consciousness. You are still on the concrete floor but you're soaking wet and everything smells like damp cement. There's still a hint of puke in the air but you expected it to be more pungent. There's something else. It's faint, but it's there. Urine. You must have pissed yourself.

How long have you been out? No way to tell, but you sense the change in your environment. Water. Everything has been hosed down, the walls, the floor, your vomit and you. The blanket is heavy with it. So are your clothes. They must have just finished. You can hear a trickle flowing down through the hole in the floor, slowing to a drip as you lie there.

They slammed the door. Through the mist of your mind you heard it. It must have been what brought you around, the door being just inches away from your head.

You roll over onto your back, peeling the wet blanket from your body, and your foot knocks something over with a synthetic thud. You pull yourself up with difficulty until you are sitting. Your hip and shoulder ache from the hardness of the floor. The pain in your head is still there, but bearable. A rag doll hanging limp, you flop your hand around to find what you knocked over. It makes contact with something and you flinch, startled. Cautious, you reach out again and your fingers find it: a bottle, plastic with a label. It's heavy for one hand but you manage to lift it and place it in your lap. There's a screw cap. You struggle with it until the seal breaks. You hold it to your nose. It smells like plastic. You stick your finger in the opening. Liquid. You withdraw and touch it to your tongue. Water. It's a bottle of water. You lift it to your cracked lips and take a large gulp, then another. Water splashes down your face as your mouth overflows. Too much, too soon, you cough.

You tell yourself to slow down, to catch your breath. The coughing continues, making your head pound again. You close your mouth to stifle the hacking and slow your breathing through your nose. It takes a moment, but you regain control. The pounding decreases to a pulse. You clear your throat and swallow the mucous. Slower this time, you drink. So good. Nothing has ever tasted this good. You swirl a mouthful around, puffing out your cheeks, separating your lips from your gums, letting it sit there before allowing it to flow down your throat.

Inhale. Exhale. Through the nose. Inhale. Exhale. Slower. Let the water do its thing. Let it get to your cells. They're howling for more. Give it to them, but not too quickly. Small sips. It tastes like life.

15

He went back downstairs to the office to ask where the son-of-a-bitch might be.

"Teachers' lounge," the secretary informed him.

High noon at the OK Corral, only it was eleven-fifteen as he swaggered down the hallway.

"Well, look who's back," came a chipper voice from behind. His old geography teacher. "All done for the year, I see?" she asked.

"All done, period. Graduated last week." He held up the padded burgundy folder, emblazoned with gold coat of arms and motto, protecting the very expensive piece of parchment.

"Oh, good for you. Congratulations. Your parents must be so proud of you."

"They came down for the ceremony, so I guess they are."

"And how's your little brother doing? Guess he's not so little anymore," she said with a look of concern.

"Grade six. He'll be your problem soon enough," he smiled.

She didn't know whether to laugh or not. "Well, so good to see you again. All the best…" she trailed off as she walked into the office.

He opened the staffroom door and walked in. He didn't knock. There was the son-of-a-bitch, lounging on a beat up couch with his feet up on the coffee table next to his bag lunch, drinking a coffee. Crossing the room, he opened the folder and tossed it onto the coffee table. "Fu...," he began, but was foiled as, in the exuberance of the moment, the folder overshot the table and landed on the floor face down.

"What's this?" the son-of-a-bitch asked as he leaned over to pick the folder up from the floor.

"My diploma." Making those words sound smug through the embarrassment of missing the table was impossible. The son-of-a-bitch examined the diploma, nodding his head. Then, he did the unthinkable. He looked up from the parchment, made direct eye contact, and said, "I knew you could do it," with a smirk, before taking a swig of his brew.

The graduate stood dumbstruck. How many years had he yearned for this moment? How many times had he opened up the little box inside him to hear the echo of those words, "You're never gonna make it," when he needed motivation to push ahead. The wind physically left his sails. "But you said...," he stammered.

"I know what I said. You just needed a good swift kick in the ass. You're welcome." He handed back the diploma and grabbed the brown paper bag from the table. "Now get out of here. I'm having my lunch."

Bastard.

16

I spent, what I believe to be, a whole day counting seconds, one Mississippi after another, until I could no longer stay awake. Fourteen hours and forty-seven minutes of Mississippis is a hell of a long time, fifty-three thousand two hundred and twenty, to be precise. Not precise. I'm sure my pace was inconsistent, but it's the one day since I've been here that I'm sure was a day, whatever that is.

What is time? How do we mark it? It certainly marks us. What is a day, a month, a season, or a year?

Breakfast, lunch, and supper: three meals a day. Another way we mark time. Eggs, cereal, toast, or pancakes is breakfast. Soup, sandwich, or salad is lunch. Oh, the variety supper brings. Not here. They slip food into my cell when I'm sleeping. Usually, it's rice with some minimal bland protein thrown in. I'm never sure which meal it is. I never know how long I sleep. I just sleep when I am no longer awake. I am awake when I am no longer asleep. These states are pretty much the same, spent alone in darkness.

I once watched an educational show on TV with my middle daughter a while ago. Neil deGrasse Tyson was talking about how time is measured. The explanation was fascinating. Time is a construct established to measure movement through space. A day is a planetary revolution. A season is a tilt on an axis. A year is a circle around a star. An hour is a division of a revolution; a minute, a division of an hour; a second, a division of a minute... on Earth.

Time is a circle, not a line.

Time alone in the darkness is hell.

17

You squeeze your eyelids tight, hoping for some specks of colour to form as they usually do - as you did when you were a child – waiting to see the beautiful ring explode on your retinas, then linger, eyes open, creating an aura around the objects of your sighted world. Nothing. No flecks. No circle of light. Only tar.

The sips of water are doing their thing, rehydrating.

The wet of your clothes irritates your skin. The material's rough and itchy to begin with, sack cloth, but the damp fibres feel as if you've been sitting in a bathing suit for too long. It's not warm. It's not cold. It's not just right, it just is. You pull the shirt off over your head. The air is a cat's tongue, but it's better than the sucking cloth. You wiggle out of the pants, one spongy glute at a time, then strip them from your legs inside out. You drop the clothes beside the blanket.

Naked is better. There's nowhere to hang it all to dry. Or is there? You are still not sure of the lay of the land.

You are at the door. You know it is not tall, over a yard. Your hand guides you up the door as you rise to your feet slowly, but you know the ceiling is low. You have a scrape on your head to prove it. The roof curves inward from the exit. You follow the curve to find its highest point. You have no sense of balance and if you let go of the ceiling, you know you will topple. You mind your step, feeling your way with your toes to avoid the hole in the floor. There it is. You hook the toes of one foot over its edge. You are still hunched over with your hands above you, mapping the ceiling. At the highest point, there's an opening. You feel a slight movement of air coming from above. Ventilation. Your fingers don't move far. Criss-crossed metal covers the one-foot hole. Rebar. It has the texture of rebar. Not much space in the grid-work, an inch maybe, just enough for two fingers. The ceiling is less than five feet off the ground. You cannot stand up straight nor can you touch the ceiling at the centre when on your knees.

You kneel down to examine the opening in the floor. It feels like the one above, minus the rebar. You lie on your stomach and reach down. The hole goes deeper than the length of your arm, or your scratched up leg from when you discovered it. Drainage.

How wide is your cell? With your fingers over the edge of the drain, lying on your stomach, you stretch your body across the floor, trying to reach the wall or the door with your feet. Not quite. You lift your body up into a pushup and shift about a foot until your toes touch concrete, maybe eight feet from wall to drain.

Now for the walls. You start at the door where you left your wet items and pad your way down, looking for the corners. Ten feet from the door and you've yet to find an adjacent wall. Twenty feet, still nothing. This is not computing in your mind. Your cell cannot be this big. Thirty feet, forty feet, still no corner. Another ten feet and your fingers hit vertical metal. It's another door. You wonder how this can be. The way sound bounces off the walls your cell has to be smaller. With the next step your foot finds something: damp wool. You bend down to touch it and realize you have found your wet blanket and clothing.

"What?" you ask aloud. "How...?"

A circle. You've gone in a circle. There *are* no corners. You have imposed the corners in your mind because you cannot see, but the cell is round and domed, like a very short silo. You don't know why, but you feel better in the knowing, in the understanding of your environment.

Now, what about your clothes? How can you get them dry? It's another problem to solve.

Your mind goes back to the opening overhead. You can hang your clothing from the rebar if you stuff it through. With items in hand, you step to the centre but your foot sinks into something. It's spongy. You set your clothes down and secure whatever it is with your hand while you extract your foot.

Bread. It's bread, two pieces together. You peel them apart. The substance between the slices feels like cheese, the square, individually wrapped, single molecule away from plastic kind: a sandwich on a soggy paper plate. You eat.

Water and food; it's a good day.

Other days won't be as good.

18

    His little brother was more than anyone, especially his parents, had expected. They had tried to have a baby for a few years but to no avail. They thought having a second child would be nice, but if it wasn't in the cards, that was fine, too.

    The one they had was a joy. As a baby, he had been an easy first child. Before long he was on a regular schedule of eating and napping, and by four months of age he was sleeping from ten o'clock to six in the morning. His parents were thrilled that he hit all of his milestones ahead of time and was a bright little light. His mother read to him every night and his father taught him how his hands could manipulate tools to fix and build things out of metal or wood. He was never a difficult child at home or at school.

    If the first child was this easy, who wouldn't want a second? But the second never came and as time went on, the possibility of conception slipped away from their reality and then from their hopes.

    A few months before his tenth birthday, he noticed his parents having very serious conversations just out of earshot and his mother was seeing a doctor more than usual. His young mind went to worst case scenarios. Other kids at school had lost parents and grandparents to a variety of illnesses and from what he heard from them, his mother and father were showing similar symptoms of impending doom.

He didn't know how accurate his suspicion really was. One Saturday evening, after his parents had spent the day with him doing all the things he loved to do, they sat down with him on the living room couch. This was a sure sign of a looming serious conversation. It was how he had found out about the passing of both grandparents and of the decision to put the family spaniel to sleep after fifteen years of life.

"Honey, Dad and I have something to tell you," his mother said with an awkward smile.

"Who's dying? I think it's you," he said to her as a matter of fact.

"Dying? No. No one's dying. Why would you say such a thing?"

"We're sitting on the couch together. We never sit on the couch together unless it's about death."

His father started to chuckle. "No one's dying, son. Actually, it's the opposite. We're having a baby. You're going to be a big brother."

He remembered thinking at the time he would have preferred another death conversation. "I don't need a brother."

"Or a sister?" his mother asked. "Oh come on. It will be great having a baby sister."

"Or brother," his father jumped in.

"I like it the way it is, just the three of us."

"Honey, I know it's going to be a big change in all of our lives, but you'll see, it will all be just fine. Trust me."

It was not fine. The pregnancy was difficult for his mother, who was now thirty-nine years old; two years older than his father. He remembered she spent much of her last trimester either in bed or lying on the couch.

The baby still did not want to come out a week past the due date, so they scheduled a caesarean section. His brother had yet to be born, but was already creating challenges for his parents.

He told himself the reason they named the baby after his father was due to a lack of imagination associated with their ages. The reality was he did not understand why the baby was getting his father's name. Didn't that right belong to the firstborn? Any other kid he knew who had his father's name was the firstborn.

The first six months of Junior's existence were terrible. He was a restless baby, in continual motion, and would not take naps. When he did, it was only for half an hour at a time. Evenings, from eight o'clock until two were filled with wailing, as Junior was extremely colicky.

His parents traded off sleeping schedules so each might get some rest. His father, who worked at the mill from eight until four, spelled off his mother for a couple of hours to get dinner on the table and eat, then he would try to sleep from seven until eleven. He would then pack Junior up in the car and drive around town until the baby fell asleep. If his Dad was lucky, he might be able to catch a couple more hours of sleep before work.

His mother slept from eleven until seven. His father thought this a fair arrangement because she had to care for Junior all day. Besides, his father was a night owl who usually only slept for five hours a night.

Junior was a bottle baby. Anyone could feed him, anyone except for his older brother. Junior must have sensed the resentment. He fussed even more whenever his brother helped out with feeding, changing, entertaining, or distracting. The tone for their brotherly relationship was set for life.

So went the rest of the year. The parents spent little time together and did not sleep in their bed simultaneously. As for the firstborn, he was left to his own devices. He begrudged Junior's existence, stealing his parents away from him just by being born. He rarely saw his father except for dinner and weekends, and by the time the weekend did roll around, his parents had no energy to spend on him. He was glad for school and became involved in many different organized activities just to keep out of the house. He was the child the parents never had to worry about, the responsible one.

Junior was a thrower, a hitter, and a biter. To give herself a break, his mother took him to different mom and baby groups in town. However, the other parents, fearing for their own children's safety, discouraged her from returning.

When Junior learned to walk and talk, the trials for the family grew exponentially.

Living in a company town has its challenges. Most of the people were blue collar folk with minimal education under their hardhats, good people working hard to make a living and raise their kids the best they could. A few fell into the category of ignorant and rude. One foul-mouthed twenty-something couple lived across the street. The husband and wife, who both worked at the mill in different capacities, wrapped up their working days by crashing on a throw-away couch on their front porch with a case of beer. The more they drank, the louder and more belligerent they became with each other. Argument was the foundation of their marriage, and profanity was the mortar for their arguments. Each evening after dinner the four-letter jabs and crosses would drift across the street to fall upon young ears.

His mother was not impressed and insisted that her husband go across and "give them a talking to." His father was not a confrontational man. He preferred to let things run their course without making waves. He made decisions in his own home and at work, but when it came to the rest of the world, he preferred to keep his head down. His angry mother went over and gave them a piece of her mind, but a few days later, the swearing returned in earnest. His mother was not going to win this battle. The couple reminded him of a fable his parents had once told him involving a scorpion.

Some of the profanity had made an impression on Junior and the words flew out of his mouth at the most inopportune times. One Saturday evening when the boy was five, the family went out for dinner to a local restaurant. When the waitress was taking their orders, she looked at Junior with a genuine, kind smile and asked, "And what would you like to eat for dinner tonight, cutie?"

"I'll have a hangaberger, bitch."

His parents were mortified. At the age of fifteen, being interested in making a good impression with nineteen-year-old waitresses, he was humiliated.

His mother's constant efforts to correct her young son's foul mouth backfired on her. She and the two boys were standing in line at the grocery store, Junior in her arms. He was looking over her shoulder at the woman behind them. As strangers are wont to do with little children, the woman waved her fingers to him and said, "Hello." Junior waved back and said, "Now don't you say fuck. Fuck is a bad word."

They left the store at a brisk pace, his mother's eyes to the ground.

When he was old enough, his parents asked him to baby-sit his little brother every other Saturday night so they could play bridge at their friends' house, wanting to return to some sense of adult normal. He was not receptive to the idea.

"You actually want to leave us alone together in the same house? Are you out of your minds?"

But his parents were becoming desperate for some time to themselves. When they offered him twice the going rate for sitters he reluctantly agreed. His mother left a list of activities Junior could be distracted by if he became restless, one of which was banging on pots and pans with wooden spoons. A side note on the list said that this activity was something "he can do for hours."

Within fifteen minutes of his parents' departure, Junior was restless. He had already lost interest in playing with his toys. Instead, he was trying to toss them into a hanging glass light in the hallway, imagining the ceiling fixture as a basket into which he was throwing balls. This would not end well. When he tried to intervene before glass came shattering to the floor, his rambunctious brother made him the new target. A metal Hot Wheels car caught him on the eyebrow, opening the skin.

He knew that pummelling the little boy would not solve his problem. To be honest, he was quite afraid of Junior whose unpredictability was his greatest weapon.

Instead, after staunching the blood flow from his wound, he went to the kitchen, opened the cupboard, and emptied all the pots and pans onto the floor. "You wanna come to the kitchen?" Junior didn't need to be asked. He was in the doorway within seconds of hearing the metal hit the tile. He grabbed two wooden spoons from the drawer and arranged the cooking implements from smallest to largest, left to right. Sitting cross-legged in front of them, he started bashing away. He really liked to hit things. An hour later, Junior was still beating out rhythms, and did not seem the least bit tired, so his big brother sat in the living room with his Discman replacing the banging noises with the soothing sounds of Iron Maiden in his headphones. That night was the best they had ever gotten along. Future Saturday nights would not turn out as well.

His parents hoped that Junior's attendance at school would give them respite from the constant supervision. Not exactly the case. True, he was out of sight, but never out of mind. Then came the phone calls followed by meetings with administration, teachers, and counsellors, and appointments with psychologists and other specialists to figure out how to best serve this filterless, impulsive child.

Ritalin was prescribed, the fix-it-all drug of the education system. Doses were altered over time in order to achieve the right fit. Some weeks were better, others were worse. When the doctors finally decided upon the proper amount and frequency for optimum effect, Junior became a manageable empty shell with no affect. He did what he was told to do at school, but had no investment in doing anything. His spark and his personality had vanished.

He referred to this as his brother's "zombiefication". He liked Junior this way.

His parents felt guilty. This was no longer their little boy, so full of unbridled energy and commitment to each moment, and they felt responsible for stealing his true spirit. It was his mother's decision, after one month of relative peace in the house, to take Junior off the meds. and his father reluctantly agreed. Of course, the elder child had absolutely no say in the matter, but at seventeen, he was close to getting out of Dodge and leaving his family to fend for themselves without him, not that they would even notice he was gone. When you do what you are supposed to, and never bring conflict or trouble with you, you are invisible.

19

Words are all I have here. Even memory falls to words to give context to the images.

There are words not written on the page, not spoken in the moment, not sung to the music. Words offered into the space between people make us vulnerable. Once committed to the medium, they are forever there, at least until the medium is destroyed or dies.

We are mediums, our minds and our memories, yet we are also the most unreliable of sources. We believe we hold the truth of our experience, but everyone's truth is different. We alter truth to fit our interpretation of a situation, to make it palatable or more memorable. Fourteen eye witnesses to a crime and no two stories are alike, yet they all spoke the truth, their truth. Even evil believes it is righteous.

What of the unspoken, the words we didn't say but should have? How much of our lives are lived in the words abandoned? Musicians understand the power of a rest, the silence between the notes. The words not spoken are often more telling than those that are.

And there are the words you didn't need to say, where a

simple look fulfilled the meaning when words could never suffice. My mother had so many looks that said more than her words ever could. My father had a few, but he was much more subtle. My wife has some doozies, most of them negative. She used to have a beautiful one she gave to me in the beginning, but it has long faded away. Where did it go?

In this sightless void I see flashes of moments past, expressions on faces saying so much more than the words lost in my mind to the sickle of time. I also hear the words I should have said but never did, and the words I yearned to hear but never heard.

20

University brought him freedom in many ways. He was no longer continually associated with his troublesome brother; he was no longer labeled as the son of a manager at the mill; and, he could re-invent himself if he wanted to. He continued to be studious. Although he still thought journalism would be a good career choice, he had decided to broaden his experience of language and style by immersing himself in English Literature. He worked hard at his courses, spending timeless solitary hours reading, and then preparing essays. He really enjoyed completing the writing assignments. Also, after he had been exposed to the broader cultural experiences of a big city, he developed a fascination for the paintings in nearby art galleries. Occasionally he let his already-thinning hair down with a night on the town with compatriots from his classes. Even then, he was the responsible one, drinking only to get a little buzzed, but never to the point of relinquishing control to drunkenness, and making sure his intoxicated companions made it home safely.

He was attracted to women who were out of his league: his physical appearance did not meet university standards of a prize catch and his sometimes grating personality lead to the utterance of unwarranted opinions. He adopted his dating philosophy from Shakespeare: "Sell while you can; you are not for all markets." If a woman showed interest in him, he went for it whether he liked her or not. Women interested in him were few and far between.

During the summers he avoided home, always choosing to find work in the city. His father had offered to get him a job at the mill each summer. "The money's good and you can live at home and not pay rent," he would say. However, he declined this option, having sworn to himself he would never end up at the mill under any circumstance.

While he was completing his last year of postsecondary, his father came down to the city for a weekend environmental conference, all expenses paid by the company. They went out for dinner together, the first time they had been alone with each other since Junior was born. They both felt the awkwardness of strangers as they sat across from each other in the restaurant at the Ramada Inn where his father was staying.

After they had each ordered a beer and a steak, he suddenly realized he had never seen his father drink before. It was even stranger when his father ordered two more over the course of the meal.

"How are things going back home?" A relatively safe question to get the conversation out of neutral, he thought.

"Oh, good. Same old, same old."

"Mom's good?"

"She's good."

He didn't ask about Junior.

"So, graduating this year. What's next?"

"I've been sending out my resumé to small town newspapers, big ones, too, but those chances are pretty slim. If

I can get into a small publication I can get some experience under my belt."

"Good plan."

When their meals arrived they ate in silence. His father finished the last of his steak and took a drink from his third lager to wash it down. "I've always been real proud of you, you know."

This unexpected praise stunned him

"Thank you. I've worked hard."

"I know you have. Always so independent and responsible."

"I didn't think you'd noticed."

His reply caught his father off guard. "What do you mean? I've noticed. You've always been a great kid. Never caused your mother or me any concern. It's just…"

"I know. Junior."

"He's just needed us much more than you ever did. We've had to work so hard just to keep him from going off the rails with everything."

"And how's that going?" he asked, not really wanting to know.

His father took a moment to think his answer through. "Not great."

"So, really is same old, same old back home. What now?"

"He's just not doing well with school, skipping class all the time and getting into fights when he is there. Mom caught him smoking last week. He's twelve years old, for Christ's sake." He took a long pull from his beer. "I think he's smoking other stuff, too."

"Jesus. What are you going to do?"

"What we usually do, I guess. Just keep trying. He'll come around eventually."

"Or end up in jail."

"He's just not cut out for school. Doesn't care for anything that happens in a classroom. Seems the only thing he likes there is music. He plays drums for the school band, has a pretty awesome teacher who puts up with his crap."

"Drums. I'm not surprised." He laughed a little, thinking back to Saturday night babysitting.

For the next two hours they drank and talked about everything, trying to cram a decade's worth of disconnect into an evening. When it came time to leave, his father gave him a hug. "I'm sorry if you felt we never paid attention to you. We *were* paying attention."

"Go to bed, Dad. You're drunk." Yet, as he walked away, wondered if the evening had been too little, too late.

21

Sometimes, in my mind's eye, I remember my life in first person. I recall the events through my own eyes. In other recollections I see myself, as if through a lens, as part of the scene. I am a character interacting with the other characters and the environment. The remembrance is from the outside looking in.

Taking a break from my new job, I am driving back home for a visit along an isolated northern highway. It is autumn. I remember my hands on the steering wheel and the sleeves of my shirt. The view through the framed windshield is a strip of road running straight ahead in front of me, the sides of the asphalt converging in the distance. I am surrounded by Group of Seven landscape under overcast sky with a fine mist lingering in the air. I see the wiper blades intermittently sweep right to left and back again, a temporary clear view.

My hand reaches for the radio dial to find a better signal as the song I'm listening to fills with static. I hear the hum of the road beneath my tires. I bring the drive-through coffee cup to my lips and breathe in its aroma as I take a swig, but it has grown cold in the hour since I bought it.

There is a sudden popping sound in front of me. A crack spider webs on the windshield, startling me. I swerve to the right, my tires catching the gravel shoulder. I step on the brakes and pull over. I am alone on the highway. I have not seen another vehicle in a long while.

I picture my hand pulling the lever to open the door before I get out to inspect the damage. Something small hit the windshield from the left of the car. I can see the angle of impact in the glass and feel it as I run my fingers across the edges. It couldn't have been a rock. There were no other vehicles around to kick one up. I scan the bush on the other side of the road, seeing only dense spruce and poplar. I remember it is October, hunting season. I think, "Did I just get shot at? Did a bullet just ricochet off my windshield?" It is the only conclusion that makes any sense. I think, "A little slower and I wouldn't have even noticed. A little faster and it would have come through the driver's side window."

The trees trigger in me a separate memory.

I see an eight-year-old boy through a camera's eye. He is me.

His father had taken their small family on a two week summer holiday to a rented a cottage a few hours north.

They ended their journey on a bumpy dirt road which led to the long narrow branch bay of a black-watered lake. Along the shoreline stood their cottage along with another dozen, all surrounded by pine, spruce, birch, and poplars.

The neighbours were a hearty francophone family of hunters and fishers who sat around bonfires until late in the evening, becoming more boisterous with the uncapping of each beer.

His father sat in an old, rustic wooden chair with a perplexed look on his face as the thick accents and *joie de vivre* rippled - then ripped - through the barrier of silent evening evergreens. Their racket drowned out the nightly news, picked up by aerial, on a black and white TV set. This was the third night in a row of late night rowdiness.

He could sense that his father wanted to tell them to be quiet as the movement of his hands began to reveal frustration. His index finger began to play with a hangnail on the adjacent thumb flicking it back and forth, over and over.

After turning off the television set, he took his young son to tuck him in for the night.

"If their noise is keeping you awake, just put your pillow over your head. It'll drown them out."

The next day, the sound of gunfire fractured the crisp dawn. Five shots, originating from the other side of the evergreens accompanied the sound of breaking glass. This must have been early morning target practice with the previous night's empties. At breakfast, the boy knew something different was about to happen in his world as his father's index finger beat a tattoo on the hangnail of the thumb to the point of bleeding. There was tension in the room. His mother sat pursed-lipped, contemplating her perked coffee until suddenly she glared at his father with her "Are you going to do something about this?" look on her face. Dressed, shaved, and loaded for bear, his father headed out the door.

"Can I come with you?" the boy asked from behind him.

"Not this morning."

"Please?"

"No." His voice was quietly stern. He wasn't upset with his son, but with the confrontation about to take place beyond the evergreens. The boy knew not to continue a verbal pursuit.

As his father disappeared into the fifty feet of spruce and pine and his mother cleared the breakfast dishes, he slipped out the door and headed toward the break in the tree line that had just consumed his father. The boy advanced quietly until he saw three men standing with his father in a clearing beside a blue-grey clapboard cottage. Between two birch trees of ample girth and height, about twenty feet apart, hung a bear. Its stomach, bared of its fur, lay open like a book with the pages hanging equally from under its splayed armpits. The bloody muscles of the abdomen had not yet been incised, but the grass beneath was clotted crimson. The bear was massive, its limbs stretching out in four directions. Its oily black hair glistened in the morning sun. The boy could not see the head lolling backwards towards the spine, away from his awestruck eyes. He had never seen anything like it, not even on TV. The sight was repulsive, yet intriguing; sickening, yet seductive. As much as he wanted to turn away, swallowing hard to keep his breakfast down, he could not pull his eyes away from the beast.

"Maudit bear, she come tru da bush..." one of the men said.

"Well, what the hell were you thinking?" his father retorted, his hands in hot fists at his side. This was the closest his father had ever come to telling someone off. The boy had never heard him swear before. His mother would not be happy if she heard what came out of his mouth.

"So, I fire tree shot an' da bear, she keep goin'. Two 'it her side. So Guy," pointing at a lanky man half his age, "'e fire two shot. Da second one fine da 'ead," the older man continued, tapping himself in the middle of the forehead with his reddened hand to illustrate the marksmanship of his younger relative. Guy stood tall with pride. From his hiding place in the brush, the boy stared at him in admiration. Bears were king of the beasts, the solitary giants roaming the forests, and this man, a mere mortal, had conquered a king – with a gun. "Wow!"

After exchanging a few more impassioned words with the older man, his father retraced his steps toward the rental, shaking his head in disbelief. Dead branches snapped under his heavy footfall.

The boy pressed his body to the spongy ground wanting to remain unseen. Yet, without adjusting his stride, his father spoke to the trees as he passed by. "Come on home. You've seen enough," and he disappeared into the maze of branches.

Disappointed that he had not concealed himself better, the boy trudged his way back in his father's footsteps.

When he entered the cottage, his father was obviously still upset. He was sitting at the kitchen table, his hands trembling slightly as he reached for his coffee cup and sipped the strong brew to calm his prickling nerves.

"Sorry, Dad." There was nothing else the boy could say.

"Go wash your hands. You've got pine sap all over them," he said as he continued to stare into the well of his cup.

"And mind your feet. I swept up as best as I could," his mother added.

The boy was standing at the bathroom sink, waiting for warmer water to come from the tap. Suddenly, he saw a flash, a little flicker of reflected light: a small piece of glass, a piece of mirror. He looked up at the medicine chest to find a rectangle of unpainted plywood where the bathroom mirror used to be. In the empty space, on the lower left side, there was a splintered hole in the wood, right in front of his face, large enough to accommodate his pinky finger as he poked at it. He turned around to where the toilet was. There was a hole right through the wall above it at the same level as the hole in the medicine chest. He could see outside light spilling through it, and beyond, the evergreens.

"What happened to the mirror?" he asked, wiping his damp hands dry on his jeans as he returned to the kitchen.

Without turning his head, his father replied, "Hunters never think about what happens to the shots that miss. Lucky none of us had to go to the bathroom early this morning."

It's like watching a movie and I cannot understand why. Shouldn't it all be through my eyes? Does the brain manipulate the memory to allow for context? And then I realize: so much of our lives are about being in the right place at the right time, or being in the wrong place at the wrong time.
Maybe the latter is how I ended up here.

22

There's a clicking sound beside your ear, inconsistent and faint. You're half asleep or half awake on the floor, naked. You drifted off after hanging everything to dry. You've spent the day pounding on the door and pleading with your captors to show themselves and to give you more food. You have also finished the bottle of water and want more.

There has been no response. You are exhausted from the effort. Your hands are sore from your futile pounding on the metal. You have also wracked your brain searching for your last memory before ending up here, but it's still too hazy, only a vague recollection of being threatened with dismissal.

There it is again, a high-toned erratic ticking, like fingernails tapping a coffee cup, but it's coming from down by your legs. Now, there's more than one. What the hell? You don't move. You strain your ears and hold your breath as you try to identify the sound and the source. You can hear your heart beating.

Something's touching your foot. It's now on your leg. Another one is on your shoulder. You bolt upright, smacking whatever is on your shoulder with your hand and shaking your leg. Too late. You are stung in both places. You have missed the one on your shoulder. Another sting, the opposite thigh, from one you didn't know was there.

"Fuck!"

You try to get away. You stand up too quickly and bash your skull on the ceiling. Back to your knees, holding your head. Now it's on the pad of your foot, behind you. You use the free foot and sandwich it between them. It stings you but you clamp your feet together in spite of the pain. You're going to kill whatever it is, no matter what. One extra squeeze and grind for good measure. You are on the floor, on your knees, panting. Your hands are at the ready to strike again. The onslaught ceases and you hear the clicking sounds retreat toward the drain hole in the floor.

You reach behind you and release your victim from the clutches of your feet and gingerly pluck it up with your fingers. It's hard to the touch. It has a shell. You poke at it with the index finger of your other hand. It's definitely dead. There's sticky liquid oozing from its side. It's two inches long and has claws and a tail.

Scorpion.

23

When he was six, he almost died.

He was playing in the backyard by himself. It must have been fall. He wore a light jacket and jeans. Between his Dad's garage and the neighbour's shed, his parents had turned a vacant space into a yard compost pile. He enjoyed building forts in the refuse of branches, dead plants, and soil in a pile which grew higher each weekend.

Beside the compost heap, at the corner of the garage, there was an old wooden barrel his father dumped grass clippings into from the rear bag of the lawnmower. It was soft and comfy in there, especially after an entire summer's clipping from the sizable lawn. He liked to take a couple of picture books from his room, climb into the barrel and get cozy, reading as the summer sun shone.

This one autumn day, he saw the potential for a new game. The refuse pile had grown over the summer and was now tall enough for him to use to access the roof of the garage. With a little struggle and some strategic maneuvering, he was able to climb up onto the rough shingles. It was a whole new world being up so high. A change of perspective to young eyes with an active imagination is like a passage to Narnia. He was no longer on a garage roof. He was in a space ship or an airplane or climbing Mount Everest.

On this day, it was the doghouse of Snoopy, his favourite Peanuts' character. Snoopy had attitude and imagination, just like he did. He wished he had a Woodstock to play with. The World War I flying ace stories were the ones he liked the most, where Snoopy's doghouse became a Sopwith Camel and he would fly through the skies in search of the illusive Red Baron. He straddled the ridge beam of the garage, a winter scarf around his neck and swimming goggles over his eyes, and flew through the skies. Through the clouds flew the Red Baron, bearing down on him from above. He zigged. He zagged. He could not shake the Baron from his tail. The enemy was firing his guns. The bullets were ripping through the Camel's wings. The engine was on fire. The plane was going down. It was time to bail out.

He leapt from the roof to soft land in the barrel. He's small. He dropped through the top ring perfectly, feet and legs sinking down through the grass. Snoopy was safe on the ground. Or was he? There was a pain in his left calf, a sudden burn, then another on his right thigh, then on his stomach. He cried out as he clamoured to free himself. Another bite in the armpit. As he tumbled to the ground, the swarm of bees rose out of the barrel and by the time he reached the safety of the back door, he'd been stung at least seven times.

He had never been stung by a bee before and his little body was on fire. His mother was in the kitchen. Between sobs, he told her what had happened. She helped strip off his clothes down to the Batman undies, then she went to the medicine chest for the Lanacane, his mother's cure-all. He told her where all the ouchies were and she smeared the greasy cream over each red blotch. There was some temporary relief. The tingles on his body began creeping up his limbs to his core. Breathing was becoming more difficult.

His concerned mother quickly redressed him. She threw on her coat, grabbed her purse, picked him up, and headed out the front door. Because she didn't know how to drive, she began to run toward the hospital, holding his bouncing body in her arms.

As they hurried through the emergency ward entrance his mother's voice panicked as she told the nurse the details. Everything was spinning and he felt as if he were breathing through a straw. The nurse lay him on a gurney and placed an oxygen mask over his face. *He sounds like Darth Vader. It's actually kind of funny. He wants to laugh.* Next, he felt a pinch in his arm as the nurse gave him a needle. Slowly, with his frightened mother sitting by his side, his chest began to open up and the tingling faded.

"A severe reaction to bee stings," will be written on his medical records from here on in.

24

Welts form at each venom sting site and your skin is numb. How many? Four? Tingles are crawling up from your toes and fingers. Your chest is getting tight and you can't catch your breath. You need help and you know it.

"Hey! Are you listening? Hey, I need help. I've been stung. Scorpions. Can't breathe." You're gasping now as you collapse onto your back. Your airway is closing quickly.

"Help." It comes out as a whisper. You are losing consciousness.

You faintly hear the door open and dampened footfall surround you. It's still black. You can't see them through your twitching eyelids. They are talking, but the voices and words are muffled as your ears fill with cotton.

There's a sharp pain in your thigh. Your eyes spring wide open, blind. Your heart is beating out of your chest as your airway suddenly clears and you take a huge gulping breath. There are fingers pressing on the side of your throat, the carotid artery, checking your pulse for a moment; then they're gone. The feet wash out the door and it slams shut.

Your breathing slows, as does your heart rate. You are

lying on your back on the concrete floor. You are naked. You are, again, alone in the darkness.

In spite of what has just occurred, all you can think is, "There are people out there and they are listening and they don't want you dead."

You cry.

25

He had encountered a scorpion only once before, at his mother's knee. She introduced him to the tales of Aesop and Grimm when he was learning to read. They had a collection of individual hardbound books, each one its own fable. He loved the watercolour illustrations. Each night before bed, she read two books to him while he followed her finger as it glided across the words. She always smelled of baby powder.

One night, as she was about to turn off his light, she asked, "Have you ever heard the story of the scorpion and the turtle?" He hadn't.

"One day," she began, "A turtle was sunning himself on the shore. As he lay there, a scorpion approached. Knowing that scorpions were dangerous, he pulled himself into his shell for protection."

"Excuse me, good sir," said the scorpion, "but I was wondering if you could do me a small favour. I really need to get to the other side of the river and, as you might know, I am not able to swim. Could you possibly take me to the other side? I could ride on your back."

From inside his shell, the turtle replied, "I know what

you are trying to do. You are trying to get me to come out of my shell so you can hurt me."

"Why on earth would I do such a thing? I have need of your services to get to the other side of the water."

"No. I think you are lying to me and I will not be fooled."

"I promise you, I have no intention of causing you any harm. It is very important for me to get to the other side. I have a suggestion. Perhaps, if I back away to a safe distance, you could get into the water and swim to the end of the log over there. I could then walk out to the end of the log and hop onto your back. This way, if I were to try to cause you any harm, you could simply go under the water and drown me."

The turtle thought about this for a moment. The solution seemed reasonable and so he agreed. The scorpion backed away, allowing the turtle to make his way into the water and to the end of the log.

"May I come out now?" asked the scorpion.

"You may," said the turtle.

The moment the scorpion was on the turtle's back, the turtle pushed off into the water, leaving the log behind.

"You promise you won't sting me?" the turtle said as their journey was underway.

"If I stung you, I would die too," assured the scorpion.

This made sense to the turtle and he was satisfied.

Yet, midstream, the scorpion stung the turtle in the back of the neck. The turtle could feel the venom begin to take effect. He started to sink, and knowing they would both drown, he gasped, "Why did you sting me?"

"It's my nature," the scorpion replied.

"Stupid scorpion," he said to his mother when she was done. "The story makes no sense."

"Maybe it will when you're older," she said.

He hated when adults told him things would make sense

when he was older. He wanted to know now, so the next day he went to his father.

"What does the story of the scorpion and the turtle mean?" he asked him.

"The scorpion and the frog, you mean?" and his father proceeded to tell his version. The frog was already in the water and didn't need as much convincing in the beginning, but the encounter ended the same way.

"But what does it mean?" he insisted.

His father was always more willing than his mother to provide straight answers. "Some people won't change - can't change - no matter how irresponsible their behavior is. It's just the way they're wired."

He still didn't understand, but he knew one thing: he was terrified of scorpions.

26

My job is to alter stories, to take someone else's words and make them better. Stories are inconstant.

It's odd how a story can change over time and depending on the teller. Perhaps it's the nature of story, to evolve in the telling, in the translation, in the relation of the narrative. This adaptation doesn't only occur in the oral tradition. Text alters from edition to edition as someone decides what remains and what is removed.

Removal, alteration, rearrangement, addition of detail: all with the goal of telling a better tale, a more vibrant account, a more engaging yarn. What words are lost in the process? What vivid metaphors and descriptions have been marred by the editor's pen, mightier than the sword?

Thomas Wolfe's *Look Homeward, Angel* was transformed by the editor's pen to be more accessible to the masses. Even the original title, *O Lost*, was too lofty. Still, it was a great novel. It was so great that the unedited *O Lost* was published on the centennial of Wolfe's birth to celebrate the original masterpiece. Was Maxwell Perkins, Wolfe's editor, wrong in doing his job so well, removing entire pages of beautiful poetic description from the manuscript?

Even a single word can become a bone of contention between writer and editor.

Smyth Publishing found one particular manuscript in its slush pile from a neophyte who might have potential. It eventually landed on my desk. It wasn't bad, but it wasn't great. After I had read it and offered my suggestions for revision to the writer, I sent him away to prepare another draft. Two months later he was back having worked his way through the numerous notes and alterations, most of which he had accepted without condition.

"There's this one note you made about the word 'wiggle' on 122. In the margin, you wrote 'sexist'," he commented as he slid the edited draft across my desk.

Because I hadn't remembered the reason, I reread the section over. "Ah, right. I recall," I smiled as I leaned back in my chair. "You are describing a business woman preparing to leave her house to attend a meeting. The word 'wiggle' infantilizes her. Female readers will find it offensive. It minimizes her."

"But isn't it what women do when they readjust a tight fitting skirt?"

"The action is not the problem. It's the word."

He came around to the side of my desk. "How would you describe this?" and he pantomimed the movement he was hoping to capture. "Is it more of a 'shimmy'? I thought 'jiggle' would be too much."

"Why is it important? Why can't you just say she 'adjusted her skirt' and be done with it?"

"Because it's real. It's a real action by a real person. I want to make her character real. It gives her dimension. She's a powerful woman who wears power clothes, but she still gives a little wiggle when she fixes her skirt in the mirror before she leaves her house, especially when no one's looking."

"But why is it important? She's not even a major character."

"I don't know, because it is. Because I've seen it." He took a moment then approached his argument from a new angle. "Is it because I'm a male writer? Would it be OK if a woman wrote it?"

Ten minutes later, after exhausting the subject, he decided it was not a hill worth dying on and conceded.

That evening, at home, my wife was getting ready to take our daughter to dance class after dinner. She stood in the bathroom and brushed her hair. I caught her out the corner of my eye through the doorway as she slipped her thumbs into the top of her jeans and pulled them up.

"Hon? What did you just do?" I asked.

She looked at me, confused. "I brushed my hair. Why?"

"No. Not what you were doing with your hair, with your jeans. What did you do with your jeans?"

"I pulled them up."

"And how did you do it? Describe it to me."

"I wiggled to get them over my hips."

"Damn."

"You're weird."

Still, I wasn't wrong. You can't second-guess yourself in the editing game or you'd never get through a manuscript. You go with your gut.

An editor is like a stage director. I am the pulse of the public, the consumer. My instincts are in tune with the world around me, walking the line between art and commerce, finding the balance while pushing the limits. The plebes of the world need exposure to more than spoon-fed jolts of simple sentences and plot without thought, but depth of thought can't be forced upon them or they'll never buy in. I look for the tipping point, just like Perkins. Yes, some moments of genius get lost along the way, but it's all for the sake of the story. The story is everything; it must be told. Yet, a story without an audience is just a whisper in the wind.

Here I am, just talking to myself, one memory bouncing off another, holding my sanity together as best as I can. A whisper in the dark.

27

You can't remember their voices. Over the last few days they've been slipping away. The harder you try to hear them in your head, the more they recede into a reverberating echo of silence.

Your family must be so worried, your wife and three daughters. More than a month must have passed, judging by your beard. You have more hair on your face now than on the top of your head.

Wherever they're holding you must be far from home. There are no scorpions where you live. You've learned how to deal with them now, you think.

You put your fingers in your ears to focus your thoughts the way you do when trying to remember the lyrics to one song when another one is playing in the car. You are desperate to hear their voices again, even if just a whisper in your mind.

The pictures are fading as well. Your time in the darkness has stolen the light from the memory's projector.

What is memory? It's not a filmstrip of your life you can just replay whenever you choose, filled with all the specific details of every moment. You don't even remember most of the dialogue. Not the specifics. There are words and pictures, usually of the high points or the low points, but life in the grey zone gets erased, or just blends in with all the other pedestrian, mundane moments of existence. Life is a puzzle with missing pieces. In the re-telling of the story, those voids are filled with creative fiction, a glue to hold it all together.

Boredom must have overcome you – you have dozed off again. As you return from sleep, your eyes see only a vastness of small pure-coloured dots: cobalt blue, emerald green, zinc yellow, vermillion... Are you still dreaming? Are you hallucinating? Is your vision damaged? You stare with incomprehension until, your retinas having gradually adjusted, you begin to discern vague shapes that move farther and farther away until your focus rests on toy ducks and flowered blankets and tiny faces with sleeping eyelids. Slowly, clarity improves until you realize that today, your memory's subject will be the births of your daughters.

"Sport". Three trips to the hospital fifteen years ago. The first one was a mistake. Your wife's contractions were painful, back labour, but they weren't close enough together. She had insisted on going and was livid when they sent you home. Ten hours later and she decided she couldn't endure any more pain, so you took her back. No birthing rooms available and the contractions still not close enough. Still not dilated. Home again. She was beside herself and took it out on you. You hadn't been insistent enough with the hospital staff. Finally, they admitted her. "Third time's a charm." Your joke was not well-received. The asshole anaesthesiologist blamed her because the epidural needle would not go in. "You need to relax and co-operate," he chastised. You wanted to deck him, especially when he kicked you out of the room until he was done.

"Einstein". You can't recall what happened twelve years

ago. But you remember thinking the ducky wallpaper border in the birthing room was ridiculous. Adults don't need little ducks on the walls and the baby's not going to give a shit.

"Princess". Seven years ago she came fast, too fast. She was crowning while the doctor and nurse were out of the room. You had to reach down and hold her head in as you yelled at the closed door for some assistance.

Primacy and regency: how the brain wires itself to conserve ROM space.

Then you begin struggling to remember more details of the middle daughter's birth, pulling at the candy floss of your mind. Your inability upsets you. You remember the wallpaper but nothing more? You try to concentrate harder on the swimming dots until the picture frames a group of student doctors coming through the door, asking if it would be all right if they watched. You telling them to get the fuck out... Or was it the fifteen-year-old's birth? Your attention wanders when all three births begin blurring together again... and... disintegrate... into confetti.

You become angry with yourself for not having paid more attention to the details of your own life. You will try again tomorrow.

The self-flagellation for forgetting the specifics is interrupted. Off to your left comes the gentle click of exoskeleton on cement. You've concluded they come from the drain. There must be other pipes feeding into the main from below and they like the dark. You've only been stung once more since the first attack. Your response was foolish. You stomped on it in a panic, not thinking about the fact your feet were bare. The reaction was not as severe as before, but breathing was difficult for a while and you could not put any pressure on your foot.

The clicking is moving closer. You are sitting on your folded blanket. Your reach behind, and your fingers find what they're looking for.

"Come here, you little shit," you say in a kindergarten teacher's voice. "Just a little bit closer. I can hear you," you sing. Your ears are your eyes. You've heard people say that losing one sense heightens the others. You know it's bullshit. They're not heightened. They're just all you've got, so you use them more.

Tick, tick. It's in front of you now, still out of reach. Will it pass by and leave you hunting for hours or retreat to its hole? It stops. It senses you and alters course toward you.

"Just a bit more," you coax as politely as your mounting adrenaline will allow. It complies.

You pounce, dropping an empty paper plate upside down atop the beast then smashing the disk with your fists until you create the crunch, but you keep pounding.

Victory! Your first kill without consequence. You are euphoric, and laughing hysterically as tears stream down your cheeks. "It's MY nature, you fuck."

Your voice does not sound like your own anymore. You are becoming someone else.

28

Our en suite bathroom faucet drips. No matter what I do, it just keeps dripping. I even paid for a plumber to repair it, but after a couple of days, it started dripping again. The sound drove me nuts when I was trying to fall asleep. I tossed and turned for hours before exhaustion consumed me. I swear the house was trying to torture me.

Jean-Paul Sartre wrote a play about being in hell. *No Exit*: three characters in a sitting room expecting to be tortured for eternity. But the torturer never comes. The true anguish they experience to atone for their sins is the misery created by the other characters, hence the quotation, "Hell is other people." I saw a production of it in university staged by the drama department. The director chose to create Sartre's hell by adding two crucial sound elements: a background Muzak soundtrack of "You Light Up My Life" on repeat, and the recording of continually dripping water. I hated the production, but I guess that was the whole idea. I could not focus on the play because of the dripping water.

I am incredibly disturbed by the fact that humans have practised methods of torture since the beginning of time; that they have devised newer and more efficient ways to make others suffer, to break their spirit. Most often the purpose is to extract information or confession from a perceived enemy.

Pol Pot's Khmer Rouge used many different brutal techniques to force prisoners to confess to treason so his regime could justify the "traitor's" execution. If a prisoner died during the interrogation, the interrogator would be executed for not having taken more care to secure the confession. American intelligence has been called out on the global carpet for the use of waterboarding at Guantanamo Bay to coerce information. The practice rarely kills, but creates the terrifying feeling of drowning. Those who have died during the application of this technique did not drown. They died from "dry drowning": a lack of oxygen, or from cardiac arrest in those with pre-existing heart conditions.

Hell can truly be other people.

It can also be isolation in confined quarters with no light, limited sustenance, and nothing to do.

"LET ME OUT!"

29

You have established a routine, a pattern, to give your existence meaning, purpose.

You wake. You eat the blandness they leave by the door on a paper plate. You drink the water. You exercise.

This is a new addition to your life. Other than riding your bicycle when the weather permits, you have never been one to exercise. You have always scorned those who spend thousands of dollars on gym memberships, home exercise machines, protein powders, pre-workout concoctions, and endless hours of lifting and pressing and squatting.

Then again, you are far from a specimen of fitness. You've made the self-deprecating joke on many occasions that you really do have a washboard stomach; it's just you happen to be doing a load of towels at the moment. It's so unfair having a beer belly when you don't drink beer. You have lost some weight, though. You can feel it in your fingertips when you do your nightly physical check for any new lumps or contusions. At least you think it's night when you do it. It's before you fall asleep.

What you do have is time. Inmates in penitentiaries

tend to leave prison more buff than when they went in if they take advantage of the yard. Hopefully, the same will happen for you.

You started with the challenge of stretching. You could barely reach your toes. You worked your way to sit-ups and push-ups, ten at a time, then twenty. You don't count the repetitions. What's the point? You just do it until you can't do any more. You do it to mark time. You do it because it's something to do.

Jumping jacks and burpees are out of the question given the ceiling height. Bicycle crunches are the closest you can get to cardio.

Today you are going to try pull-ups. The rebar on the ventilation shaft will support your weight. You know from your futile attempt to rip it from its moorings. You straddle the drain and lace your fingers through the rebar. It's not high enough to allow your body to hang at full extension, but if you bend your legs at the knees and pull your feet up behind you, you are no longer in contact with the floor. It will give your abdominals a bit of a go, but that's a good thing. You manage to accomplish two. You try for a third. It's enough for one day.

Your routine involves washing after exercise. This wasn't always the case, but one day you started noticing an unpleasant odour in your cell and couldn't figure out where it was coming from. You assumed it came from the drain into which you were voiding your bodily refuse. Upon further olfactory investigation, you came to the conclusion it wasn't originating in the drain. The smell was you. Part of your water ration was then diverted to personal hygiene, without soap, cleaning the appropriate areas with a handful of water from the daily bottle they left with your food. Pits and groin. Your breath must be hideous. Your mouth tastes awful. A daily rinse of water isn't really doing the trick; then again, there's no one to breathe on.

"Afternoons" are devoted to plotting your escape. You run different scenarios in your mind, mapping your way through as many as possible "what-ifs" as you can come up with. You have arrived at a plan, but it's too soon to implement it. You will have to be in better physical condition.

You've also been using this time to figure out the why. Why were you taken captive? You've made a list of all the people you've pissed off in the world: wife, brother, students, writers, workplace associates. You wrote articles for a small local newspaper at the beginning of your career, but those were all human-interest stories and local event reporting, nothing investigative causing any controversy. No, you had to give up on investigative journalism. No one on the list had the wherewithall or means to do this.

Next you ponder whether to believe this was a random act... but to what end? Ransom? You barely make ends meet. Your inheritance went into your mortgage. Neither you nor your wife is related to anyone with cash flow. Information? You have none you're aware of. Besides, no one has had any contact with you to interrogate you. Some days, you wish they would. At least it would be something. On a very bad day you even entertained the idea of an alien abduction. Sadly, this theory remains the most plausible.

"Evenings" are for memories. This is the most challenging time. You thought it would be easy, but reflection can cut both ways and the focus required is exhausting. The exhaustion proves beneficial as sleeping usually follows. You realize you haven't had any dreams. You think it odd, but nothing about this place makes any sense.

30

His father worked at the mill in management, overseeing environmental standards long before that practice was chic. He was a scientist of intellect whose head was filled with data and statistics, not to mention a precisely memorized table of the elements. He committed everything to memory and never took notes.

Early retirement was probably the worst thing that could have happened. It was as if all the information in his head no longer had a use and, needing a way out, it started feeding upon itself.

Witnessing a man whose brain is a fortress develop early-onset Alzheimer's is devastating for a family. Being the son of that man is looking into your own genetic future with trepidation.

The illness crept its way into their world as lost words in the middle of sentences. Simple words his father usually tossed about effortlessly became elusive. The resulting frustration erased even more vocabulary.

These symptoms began to manifest themselves within the first year of early retirement. The company had offered him a package. It including a full pension after twenty-seven years of service. The offer was a means for the company to reduce expenses by letting the highest wage earners go before sixty-five.

Although his parents managed to travel for a few months before early signs of dementia developed, these weren't the golden years they had been anticipating.

During their first spring of freedom, they drove down to see the grandkids. He hadn't seen his father in close to a year, not since the retirement party the previous summer. Junior hadn't been able to attend.

They had all gone out for dinner at a downtown pub. As his father was ordering bangers and mash, his eyes widened when he forgot what he wanted to order. The menu was open in front of him and his finger was pointing at the words, but he could not process the letters he was pointing at.

"Dad wants the bangers and mash," he jumped in, "and a pint of Guinness, right Dad?"

"I can order my own damned food," he snapped.

"Sorry, I was just…"

"I'll have the bangers and mash and a Guinness," he rattled off to the server and slammed the menu shut.

The older two granddaughters were startled. They had never heard their Grandpa use so harsh a tone. The eldest leaned over to Grandma and whispered, "Is Grandpa OK?"

"Oh he's fine. Just a little tired from the drive."

During the week of their visit there had been a few revealing instances of inconsistencies in his father's mind: more halted sentences of vanishing words.

One night he awoke to a noise downstairs, and when he went to investigate, he found his father sitting at the kitchen table spooning sugar into a cup of coffee, only there was no coffee in the cup.

"Dad?" he asked in a cautious tone. "What are you doing?"

"Just having my coffee before work. What are you doing here? Did you bring the girls up for a visit?"

"Dad, this is my kitchen. You and Mom came to visit *us*."

His father smiled and shook his head. "No. I've got a meeting at nine. I'm going to get dressed and go."

He put his hand on his father's arm hoping the physical contact might help reset the computer. "Dad, you're retired, for almost a year now. Let me take you back to the guestroom and you can go back to sleep. Everything will make sense again in the morning."

His father's face flushed with embarrassment as the present reality returned to him. He took in his surroundings. "You put in new countertops, I see."

"Over March break, yes."

"They look good." They nodded and smiled awkward smiles at each other. "Well, back to bed then," and off he went.

In the morning, he and his mother went for a walk.

"We need to talk about Dad," he said the second they hit the sidewalk.

"What about him?"

"You're kidding, right? He's losing words and is getting confused."

"It's called getting older. Tell me you have never walked into a room and forgotten why you went in there in the first place."

"This is different. He was in the kitchen at four o'clock this morning getting ready to go to work. That's not just about getting older."

Her eyes went to the ground as they walked and her shoulders deflated. He knew there was more to this.

"How long? How long has he been going downhill?"

"Oh, please. Downhill is a bit much, don't you think? He just gets a little disoriented in his thoughts now and then."

"How long?"

She took a breath and sighed. "He's been having some challenges remembering things for the last couple of years. It's why I wanted him to take the retirement package when they offered it. I thought the stresses of his job were getting to him and everything would be fine once he got work off his plate. He wasn't ready for it – retirement. But I convinced him." She left it there, but he could tell there was more to the story.

"Did it help? Not working?"

"Yes, it did," she said with a smile, then she added, "for a brief time, but then he became bored. We went on our trip to England, but being in a strange place just confused him. He was fine most of the time we were there, then he'd start getting lost, thinking he was back home."

"Mom, why didn't you say something to me?"

"You are five hours away and you have your own family to deal with, especially now, with the baby, and Lord knows your hands are full with that wife…" She caught herself mid-sentence. It was no secret his parents did not approve of his spousal choice. Because they had always thought he could have done so much better and, given her difficulties, they really showed their disenchantment when he had announced child number three was on the way.

"Does Junior know? Have you told him? He's only an hour away from you. He could come and give you a hand."

"He's been out of the country since the new year. He has a six-month contract on a cruise ship. Don't you two keep in touch?"

"Let's not go there." His brother was not a subject he ever wanted to discuss, and he immediately shifted the conversation back to its original trajectory. "Mom, maybe it's time you considered…"

"Putting him in a home? Is that what you were going to suggest? Lock him up and toss away the key just because he loses track of where he is from time to time?" There was real panic in her voice.

"It's not what I was going to say. I think maybe it's time for you and Dad to consider moving here. Sell the house and get a little condo close by in town. Then I can help with things. We have a great hospital here in partnership with the university where they do research on dementia. I was just reading something in the paper last…"

"Our house is the only place where he doesn't get confused. Sell it and move here? It won't do any good for him at all. No. It is not an option." She was adamant, and when Mom dug in her heels, it was time to move on.

Two months later his mother called early one morning. She was weeping.

31

I don't cry anymore, at least not lately. I cried myself out early on, I suppose. There are only so many tears allotted to any given tragedy. I don't seem to have any left. Tears are a symptom of being out of control, as far as I'm concerned. I haven't cried in years. In the beginning, I had no control over anything, but my tears gave them the power. Not crying is one of the only tools I have to take some power back. A school bully taught me this and I thank him for the lesson. Another instance I never told my parents about.

Wait. The last thing I remember before waking up here was riding my bike home from campus, on the path by the river. Yes, I remember now. I'd just been passed by some guy on a red Pinarello – or was it black. And then I was in the water.

Damn. Something else I have to thank the Beast for.

32

Summer holidays were for living. Each morning after his mother served his breakfast, she sent him out the door to go play in the neighbourhood. By the time he was twelve, his town was his kingdom and his yellow five-speed bike was his steed. Nobody expected him home until dinner at six. Life was perfect. He was too young for a part-time job, though he had chores to do around the house, and he was old enough to go wherever he wanted.

Unfortunately, every kingdom has its monsters. His was a year older and a foot and a half taller. He looked like a beast, with too much jaw and an overly broad forehead containing a metal plate, or so the schoolyard rumour went. "Beast" was incredibly dense in the intelligence department, and his arms were so long he could almost scratch his knees without bending over. He was always flanked by two lackeys. What is it with bullies always having at least two cronies with them? He referred to them as Dumb and Dumber and when the movie of the same name came out years later, he thought their nicknames even more fitting.

It was July and he was out riding along the bike paths by

the lake across from his house, listening to some tunes on his Walkman. He'd made a mixed tape off the radio the night before. Listening to rock music was a new addition to his preteen persona, an attempt to push his parents' love of folk music out of his brain. He still had an hour before dinner so he thought he'd take a ride out to the peninsula at the end of the park. His bike was in high gear and he was just flying along, lost in the sunshine and the rhythms of the music. As he was passing an old elm tree at the side of the path, Beast stepped out from behind it with a thick branch in his hand. He swerved to the right to avoid a collision, and as he did so, Beast speared the branch into the spokes of the front wheel. When the fork made contact with the branch, the bike flipped, launching him into the air. He went somersaulting over the handlebars and skidding down the paved path on his back. He could see the wreck of his bike lying almost in the lake. His shirt was ripped, as was the seat of his jeans, and he could feel the torn skin on his shoulder blades, elbows, and hands. He was sure he had cracked his tailbone.

After Dumb and Dumber appeared from behind some bushes, the trio of bastards had one hell of a laugh in between taunts and jeers. When the shock of the impact had worn off, he started to cry as the pain set in. His assailants laughed even harder.

"Listen to the little baby," Beast mocked in a tone all bullies learn from the handbook. "You better run home to mommy. She'll kiss all your boo boos," and they roared hysterically.

Dumber was cackling so intensely he could hardly breathe. Everything escalated. The more they laughed, the more he cried. The more he cried, the harder they laughed. He tried to sit up but the intense pain resulted in his bawling uncontrollably.

Somehow, Beast formed a new idea in his tiny brain. "Aw, look at him. He's all dirty from his fall. We can't send him home dirty, now can we?" and he nodded to his buddies, who gradually understood the gist of his intentions. Dumb and Dumber grabbed his arms, and Beast, his feet. After carrying him over to the side of the lake, they started swinging him back and forth.

"And-a-one, and-a-two, and-a-threeeeeee," and they tossed him into the water.

By the time he slogged his way onto shore, they had disappeared. He sat in the muck beside his bike, the front wheel twisted into some hideous piece of contemporary sculpture, and continued to cry so gutturally he threw up all over the shore. Finally, after dragging his bike home and tucking it inside the garage, he went into the house through the back door.

"Oh my God! What happened to you?" his mother yelled when he came into the kitchen, but she immediately became too distracted to hear his response. Junior, now two years old, and in mid-tantrum, was throwing toys around the room and at his mother.

He tried to answer her over the existing din, "I had a big wipe out and ended up in the lake."

"Sorry? What?" she asked, ducking to avoid a flying Mr. Potato Head.

"I had a wipe out and I – never mind." He headed up the stairs to strip off his torn clothes and tend to his injuries in the bathroom. The battle continued downstairs as he washed out the cuts and scrapes as best he could, then clenched his teeth as he dabbed peroxide on the wounds. They stung like hell. Trying to reach the cuts on his own back was challenging, but he managed. He would have gratefully appreciated help and sympathy from his mother, but these days parental assistance was rare.

He was still in the bathroom when his father returned from work and stepped in to help his mother. He could hear tense, mostly indiscernible, voices below, but he did make out his father saying, "...well where is he and why isn't he helping you?" He figured his mother provided the answer because when he finally went downstairs after things had settled down, his father commented, "Heard you had an accident. You OK?"

"I'm fine." They all sat down to dinner.

The next day, he went to the hardware store to spend his allowance money on a new front wheel and tire for his bike. As he sat in the garage using his father's tools to make the repairs, he stared at the twisted rim and snapped spokes. "I'm never going to cry again," he promised himself.

He never did, not even at his father's funeral or at his mother's a year later.

Beast wasn't done with him yet, or rather he wasn't done with the Beast.

33

His mother was so upset on the phone that he couldn't understand her at first.

"Mom, you have to calm down. Is something wrong with Dad?"

She started babbling so much he couldn't understand her words through her tears until she got to, "...and then he hit me."

"Slow down. He hit you? Are you OK? Start over again."

Calming herself, she explained what had happened. "I was awake before him this morning and I got out of bed to go to the bathroom. I must have woken him up. When I tried to get back in bed, he wouldn't let me. He started yelling, "Who are you and why are you trying to get in bed with me? I'm a married man," and then he pushed me away. I tried to explain I was his *wife*, but he would have none of it. I told him he was being ridiculous and slipped back under the covers. Then he hit me, a slap across my face, more than a slap."

"Where is he now?"

"He told me if I wouldn't leave the room, he would. He's down in the kitchen. I'm afraid to leave the bedroom."

"Is there anyone you can call to come over? Is Junior back in the country? Can you call him?"

"No. He's still away. I guess I can call one of the neighbours."

"Good. I'm jumping in my car right after I hang up. I'll be there as soon as I can."

When he arrived five hours later, he found them both sitting at the kitchen table, dressed, and having lunch. His father was back in his right mind and they were chatting away as if nothing had happened, but something definitely had. His mother's cheek was bruising up and there was swelling along the jawline.

His father was surprised to see him. But when he made eye contact with his mother, she was shaking her head with a very stern look on her face, a non-verbal "don't say anything about it," he had seen many times before, usually regarding his brother.

"What brings you to town?" his father asked as he stood and crossed the floor to shake his son's hand.

"I'm – meeting up with a new writer who lives in a cottage just north of here. Thought I'd stop in and say hello."

"Oh, who's the writer? I might know him."

"Oh, probably not, just moved here a few months ago from out East."

He joined his parents at the table and his mother made him a sandwich.

"See what your mother did to herself this morning?" his father asked, pointing to her bruised face.

"Goodness, Mom. What happened?"

"Wet floor in the upstairs bathroom. Had a bit of a slip, is all. Caught my cheek on the sink." Her covering lie gave him an idea.

"You know, I've been thinking maybe it's time the two of

you started thinking about downsizing. I think the old house is getting to be a bit much for the two of you. Maybe you could move into something with just one storey, then you wouldn't have to worry about stairs, and you certainly don't need two bathrooms anymore."

His mother followed the lead. "We were just talking about that a couple of weeks ago, weren't we, dear?"

The look in his father's eye said he had no recollection of the conversation, but he also did not want to admit to not remembering something. "Well, yes we were," he agreed.

"Maybe you would like to be closer to your grandkids so you could see them more than once or twice a year. The girls would love that. You'd be there to watch them grow up, and we could help you out with things if you ever needed it."

"It's an interesting idea," said his father, "but your mother is involved in so many things in town. I don't think we're ready just yet."

"Well, it was just a thought. Better to do it now, though, while you're both still in good health. The move would be tougher to do if either of you became ill. Imagine if Mom's fall this morning had been worse and she had to be hospitalized. There would be no one around to help you out, Dad."

"We do have friends, you know."

"It's not what I meant."

His mother chimed in, "Maybe we should think about it. It would be so nice to see more of the girls."

"But what about all your – your..." The word would not come and the waiting silence became awkward. "Oh, damn. What's the word I..."

"What about all my volunteer work?" she said. "Oh, I'm sure I can find plenty of things to volunteer for in a new place."

"Why don't you drive down for a visit at the end of the week and spend the weekend? We could look at a few places close by. I think I saw a cute little house up for sale in our neighbourhood, and there's the condo complex over on Highland, right across from the mall."

"Oh, I'm not sure," his father grumbled.

"As I said, it was just a thought." One thing he knew about his father: no matter his state of mind, unless it was his idea, he probably wouldn't go for it. The other thing he knew for certain was his father would do anything for his mother. "I was just thinking of Mom's safety."

"Well," his father relented, "I don't think we have any other plans this weekend. Maybe we could come down for a visit."

His mother gave her son another look, this one of relief shining in her eyes as she nodded in affirmation.

So began the onerous process of relocating. During a two-week visit they successfully ended their search for new accommodations by finally settling on a third-floor condominium relatively close to his house. He had previously convinced his parents that they would be better off without yard maintenance and snow removal. His mother was delighted with their new home, which was easily accessed by elevator. His father was attracted by the building's well-equipped basement workshop where he could spend time on his latest woodworking projects – creating a Victorian style dollhouse for each of his granddaughters. The third-storey location would become a critical issue latter on, but no one anticipated its significance at the time.

When his parents returned to the northern town where they had spent all their married lives, they put their home on the market and began the overwhelming task of sorting, discarding, and packing a lifetime's accumulation of family treasures. He became invaluable to his parents both during and after the move. Any free time he once had was now consumed with getting them resettled.

Demands on his time increased even more when his father was no longer allowed to drive after a trip alone to the grocery store.

When leaving the parking lot, he mistakenly turned right instead of left and became lost in an unfamiliar part of town. His frustration caused distraction and he ran a red light. After swerving to avoid hitting a pedestrian at a crosswalk, he drove the car into a high curb, damaging the front wheel. When the police arrived to assist, his father was blathering to himself incoherently, unable to say with any certainty where he was or what year it was.

The accident was oddly fortuitous. It forced his father to admit he was experiencing some diminished capacity and needed medical help. It also resulted in the suspension of his driver's license until he could present a medical certificate stating that he was fit enough to operate a vehicle. This was never going to happen.

After he had sold the car at his mother's behest, he was forced to take on an additional role in his parents' lives. He made time in his own schedule to chauffeur them on personal errands, to weekly grocery shopping, and to ever-increasing medical appointments. Assisting his parents, dropping his daughters at three different schools in the morning, driving Sport to soccer and volleyball games, Einstein to Girl Guides and coding classes, Princess to dance and vocal lessons, his own comings and goings for work: he was spending more time in his car than anywhere else. Despite feeling the additional pressure, he helped out with a smile and not a hint of disdain. After all, he was the responsible one.

There were increased incidents related to his father's deteriorating mind. He arrived at the condo one morning to find his mother mopping up orange juice from the floor.

"Did you have a spill? Here," he said, getting down on his knees beside his mother, "let me help."

Her face told him it was more than a spill, and so did her words. "He asked me to bring him some orange juice, so I did. He looked at the glass and told me it was milk and started to raise his voice accusing me of trying to make him think he was losing his mind. Then he threw the juice in my face and stormed off to the bedroom. That's where he is now."

A month later his mother phoned him. She was very upset. "Can you go pick up some means of locking the sliding door to the balcony and install it for me?"

"Sure. Did someone try to break in?" he asked.

"Your father woke up in the middle of the night thinking the apartment was on fire and dragged me out onto the balcony to get away from the flames. He was trying to push me over the side to save me. If I hadn't slapped him across the face, he'd have pushed me over the rail for sure. It's thirty feet up!"

The doctors strongly suggested her husband needed more care than his mother could provide. With their guidance, she added his name to a waiting list for a seniors' facility, but the way the system worked, his mother had no choice as to which facility. She listed her top three preferences, which were the ones in closest proximity to where they lived, but the expected wait time for a bed to open up in any of them was at least eight months. His mother was beside herself with anxiety. His father was becoming more unpredictable each day and she feared for her safety.

"I just don't know what to do. He's still in there, somewhere. Some days he's his old self and you wouldn't think there was anything wrong, but then he'll lose himself and get angry."

"We just have to wait it out until a bed becomes available. It's all we can do."

"But I'm afraid of him," she blurted out.

His parents had been together for a long time. They had faced so many challenges and had survived them together, stronger than before; and now his mother lived in fear of the man whom she had loved so effortlessly for decades.

The realization that she had been losing a little bit of her husband each day for the last three years made him sad. He began to assess his own marriage, one in which the challenges had resulted over time in their disconnection. He felt himself beginning to well up but pushed the tears away.

"We'll just have to do the best we can. We'll be fine. Trust me." He tried to be reassuring.

"He's missing!" Her voice was panicked on the phone. "I walked to the library to renew a few books, and when I returned, he was gone. I was away only fifteen minutes. I told him where I was going. He's not even dressed and he didn't take his coat."

"Have you called the police?"

"No. I thought you could come over and we could go looking for him."

"I'm in the middle of…. All right. I'm on my way, but call the police and tell them what's happening."

As they were searching the neighbourhood, his cell phone rang. The police had, indeed, found his father wandering the streets downtown in his pajamas, slippers, and bathrobe.

"How the hell did he get downtown?"

"Well sir, he seemed to have the wherewithall to bring change for the bus, at least that's what he told us when we asked."

"And the driver didn't think it a bit strange to see an old man in his pajamas getting onto the bus?"

"I guess not, sir. Bus drivers see a lot of weird things."

He installed a new lock on the door, one requiring a key

to unlock from both sides. His mother was a mess.

"So now I have to lock him up in his own home like some animal," she wept. "I've put child locks on all the cupboards. Child locks, for Christ's sake, just to keep him safe because he can't figure out how to open them. I just don't know how much longer I can keep this up. Have you heard anything from anyone about when they expect a bed to open up?"

"I'm sorry, Mom. Nothing. I'll call this afternoon and let them know how bad things are getting. Maybe they can bump him up the list somehow."

They wouldn't need to.

34

There is a fig tree that begins life as an epiphyte, growing on another plant when its seed germinates in a crack or crevice. Its roots reach down to the ground and envelop the host tree. For this reason, it is sometimes referred to as the "strangler fig." If more than one seed germinates, there can be several new trees surrounding the primary. As their roots spread out, they overtake the roots of the host and apply enough pressure to eventually kill it. The original tree then decomposes, providing nutrients for the surrounding vegetation, becoming columnar with a hollow central core. The new fig trees grow for years and eventually bear fruit. Then the cycle begins again. They really are quite something to see, especially when the roots flow out like ribbons for yards in all directions under a canopy which is full and lush. The view into the centre reveals a void where once its progenitor existed.

This is the description of a banyan tree. It is also an apt depiction of my wife.

Two years ago a young woman taking my creative writing course submitted a short story, a poetic allegory about her mother personified as a banyan tree. It's offspring slowly drained its life away, yet its only purpose was produce and sustain its progeny. The more mature the seedlings became, the more the parent tree died until there was nothing left but a hollow core. The story continued by exploring the fear which one of the grown seedlings experienced at the prospect of being on the cusp of bearing fruit. Would she become just like her mother?

As she read it aloud to us in the circle, my mind couldn't help seeing my wife in the story. She died a little each day as our children grew. She regretted their growth and tried unsuccessfully to hinder their progress. Her increasing insignificance and lack of influence in their lives eroded her purpose, and soon she would cease to be. Who are we without a reason?

In contrast, I revel in the development and maturation of my children, trying to encourage their independence and looking forward to each child arriving at their point of departure and self-sufficiency. Isn't that the goal of having children, to let them go out into the world, confident in having done our best in raising motivated, assured, self-determining adults?

By the time our youngest spreads her wings and leaves the nest, I'm afraid there will be nothing left of my wife.

35

Your captors have trained you well. You have learned if you are sleeping too close to the door they will not slip food and water into your cell. The first time, you tried falling asleep against the door, just to elicit a reaction, hoping to have some type of contact, but they must have felt your weight against it. The door opened briefly, then immediately slammed shut. Afterwards, you tested the waters by lying at different distances. Too close meant no food or water. Five feet away was safe. Now you make sure you sleep far enough from the door. They also know when you sleep. There's probably a microphone in the ventilation shaft.

Your daily workouts are having the desired effect. You know you have grown stronger. Fifty push-ups at a time are effortless. You can plank for three hundred Mississippis. You are even up to ten pull-ups. You have never been in such good shape. You've promised yourself you will keep up the exercise if you ever get out.

You may even be losing too much weight. You are at the tipping point. Because your body has not been receiving enough nourishment, it has begun burning fat. The food is not enough fuel to build your body. From here on in, it will start feeding on muscle. You must eat all the food they provide.

You are ready to attempt an escape. You have a plan. You think you will do it tonight.

36

A few days later his mother faced a major challenge. Her husband wanted to get out of the condo. He was feeling trapped. "I just want to go for a walk," he growled. "Can't I even go for a walk?"

"It's too cold out there right now. We'll go for a walk this afternoon when it warms up."

"I want to go NOW!" he yelled as he yanked repeatedly on the locked door. "I can't breathe in here." He turned suddenly and took a bead on his wife. "Give me the keys," he insisted as he stalked toward her in the kitchen. His gait had changed in the last few months and had become a slower, more cautious shuffle, yet the look on his face was determined. He tried to grab her by the arm, but she easily slipped away. "Give me the goddamned keys," he snapped, pursuing her in a pathetic game of cat and mouse around the living room furniture. He caught his foot on the leg of the coffee table, toppling to the floor. There was a popping sound as he landed and he bellowed in pain. His mother phoned him from the hospital to inform him of the morning's events.

The injury was a mixed blessing. A broken hip was reason enough to admit him into a care facility after being discharged from the hospital. It didn't just move him up on the list. It was his entry ticket, as there were beds available for emergency admissions.

"If I'd known that earlier," his mother said, "I'd have broken his hip myself." She wasn't serious but people say the strangest things in moments when stress turns to relief.

The institution, which was not one of his mother's three preferences, was located halfway across town, three bus rides away. The building was not well-maintained and the hallways smelled of stale urine and body odour. It was not a place in which she wanted her husband to spend what she knew were his final days.

She spoke with the administration about the possibility of a transfer to a facility closer to her home. She thought the move would be a simple matter now that he was finally in the system.

"Unfortunately, that's not the case," explained the disheveled man in a worn and ill-fitting suit who was sitting behind a weary desk piled high with paperwork. "His admission here to one of our emergency beds removes him from the waiting list for the other three facilities. If you would like me to, I can get his name back on those lists, but he'll be back at the bottom."

"This is utterly ridiculous. There must be something…"

"There's nothing I can do. It's just the way things are and I have to follow the policies…"

She did not hear the last of his explanation as she was already walking out the door, crestfallen, and down the corridor to her husband's room.

She told her son all the discouraging details when he arrived after work to see how the transfer from the hospital had gone. He felt disheartened as they sat by his father's bed. The institutional green walls were chipped and faded. The shared room's small window was hidden by the threadbare privacy curtain behind which his roommate moaned continually. They had wanted a private room in a clean and pleasant nursing home.

His father noticeably transformed in the weeks following his fall. He would be in a wheelchair from now on, never to walk again. His words became more disconnected and his voice grew weak. His eyes no longer looked outward with any gleam of hope. The mirror of his mind was now truly shattered, with missing shards. The remaining fragments reflected off each other in altered misconnected ways, memories bouncing from one to another with no linking logic, often blending different elements of recollections together into one ludicrous tale after another.

It pained him to listen as his mother kept trying to correct the memories, because her efforts only resulted in her husband's erupting frustration and despair as he stumbled his retreat along his erasing path. He and his mother had already faded into two distant and shadowy figures, withdrawing towards the edges of his father's sanity, listening helplessly as the anguished man stood alone and screamed his bootless, silent scream at a deaf heaven.

37

Churches... another image confronts me.

We were invited to dinner at the new minister's house, my wife and I. We left the girls at home. "It's nice to finally be at the point where we can leave Sport in charge of Einstein and Princess," I said as we settled in at the dinner table. "It seems I only ever use their Christian names when I am upset with them," I explained jokingly to the minister when he asked if those were nicknames.

"You never can tell these days," the pastor chuckled.

The new minister's invitation was peculiar, I thought. Usually, it's the other way around, but church matters fall within my wife's portfolio and I was just along for the ride.

We had started attending *Church of the Redeemer* just after Einstein was born. Another mother in the neighbourhood suggested a twice-a-week parent and baby group held in the church hall. I guess she had seen my wife out for a walk with the two girls, one still a toddler and the other in a stroller, and decided my wife needed some extra support. It was obvious to others she was having some difficulties.

The baby group led to regular attendance on Sunday

mornings; her involvement expanded into Bible study, a pastoral care committee, a women's auxiliary group, and then choir for the girls as they grew older. Membership provided my wife with a community where she could find some solace while struggling with whatever personal issues she was unable to resolve. I was never able to ascertain what those issues were, as she refused to discuss them with me on the many occasions I attempted to broach the subject. She seemed to have found some peace in the Lord, and I supported her on her path, though not a believer, myself.

Our former minister had been a lovely woman in her sixties whose sermons were laced with current events, literary references, historical context, ethical dilemmas and, yes, scripture. She treated the Bible as just one of many textual references in her exploration of contemporary human themes each Sunday. Scripture was not the be all, end all of source material; just another ingredient in the recipe. I enjoyed that about her. She was well-read, broadly educated, and knew how to make connections among all of the puzzle pieces. I would head home after each service feeling intellectually challenged, an accomplishment in and of itself. Unfortunately, she had retired and relocated to warmer climes.

This new padre was more by the book, the Good Book. He also manifested an annoying persona when the robes went on, shifting from the salt-of-the-earth guy-next-door off stage to the wispy solemn delivery of a human conduit for Christ himself in the pulpit. I found the man's preacher voice too holier-than-thou for my tastes, but his dinner voice and personality were genuine and earthy.

The minister's wife was an archetypal cliché of a character from a seventies' film about a peculiar Connecticut community. She was well put together, with a pleasant smile and demeanour, who happily prepared a wonderful meal for company, agreed with everything her husband said, and laughed appropriately at all of his witticisms.

Conversation during the meal covered all of the usual topics: our respective children, commentaries and observations of world events, seasonal anomalies, and geographical and vocational histories. It was typical polite dinner fare. Then came dessert and coffee in the living room.

"Getting to know the two of you a little bit more has been a real treat," he began, "especially with all the work your wife does for our congregation," he nodded and smiled toward her. She was flattered and thanked him for his kind words.

"I was wondering," he continued, shifting his gaze toward me now, "if you might be interested in giving some of your time to our Facility and Maintenance Committee. The chair informed me last week that she is stepping down at the end of the month and I haven't come across your name on any of the lists of people involved in the different groups that make *Redeemer* such a thriving community. Considering how much your wife is involved... I just thought this might be a wonderful opportunity for you to become a more integral part of the congregation. I know sometimes politics gets in the way and people end up being left out, which I'm sensing is the case with you. Please, correct me if I'm wrong."

"With all due respect, Reverend, you *are* wrong," I said. My wife elbowed me in the ribs. When I looked at her, she was giving me a wide-eyed stare and her lips were pursed. I knew the look. I turned back to the minister. "Between teaching at the college part-time, my full-time job with the publishing house, and getting my children to all of their activities, I don't have free time for volunteer work. That is why you haven't seen my name on any of your lists." I was being as diplomatic as I could, though my delivery became increasingly more staccato.

"It's just that the church could really use you," he said with a practiced warm smile. "On another matter - since you are an editor for a local publisher - I've been writing a book for the last few years, a theological guide for the twenty-first century, and I was wondering if you might be willing to show it to your..."

I had heard enough. "So, it's not just the church that could really *use* me, is it? Is this why you invited us to dinner tonight, to try to get me to champion your book, sight unseen, where I work? Trying to bribe me with some pseudo position of authority and responsibility to stroke my ego, to make me feel important just to get me to read your stupid book?"

"I beg your pardon. It was never my intention. I just thought..."

"Bullshit. You and the church are no better than anyone else. It's true: hell is empty and all the devils are here. You play politics and manipulate people to fulfill your personal agenda and justify it all in the name of Christ. You seek out the weak and disenfranchised and offer them false hope in order to rope them in. Well, I am neither, and I don't have the time for your sycophantic exploitation to get what you want." I was standing now. "You'd have been better off just asking me to give your manuscript a look-see straight up. I might have actually considered it just to be nice. I'll give you credit though, you came to the right guy because I edit fiction, which is what your book most certainly is."

I was on a roll. "I am not a believer, sir. I come to church each week with my family for my wife, for only my wife. I derive no pleasure from attending. My spirit does not feel lifted afterward. I am no more enlightened on Sunday afternoon than I was on Saturday night. I come to support my wife, who takes comfort in the service, for whatever reason. Now, we're done here. We'll see you on Sunday morning. You and I will smile at each other and offer our Sunday morning pleasantries as we always do, because that's how it works."

I headed for the door. I turned to the minister's wife and shifted my tone on a dime. "Thank you so much for the wonderful dinner." I was being genuine. "It was delicious." Besides, she was not to blame for her husband's shitty choices.

Then we left. The drive home was tense. There were no words, just glares of anger and embarrassment on her part. I said nothing. There really wasn't anything more to say.

I didn't say those exact words to the good Reverend. I certainly wasn't as eloquent. I remember saying "bullshit" and the line from Shakespeare. I remember thanking his wife for dinner and she may or may not have given me a hidden "thumbs up". I'm not sure. Maybe it's just wishful thinking. The rest of it is a reconstruction, fragments of the bricks of dialogue no one really remembers, reassembled to capture the overall idea of the possible words spoken. We're not computers with digital storage of all the bits and bytes of every single word uttered in our lives. We have to make some things up in the re-telling. We have to.

38

The October after graduating from university, he was hired by a weekly news publication in a northern community. Small town newspapers still existed at that time. The pay wasn't great, but it was a real journalism job with a legitimate newspaper. It was called The Press and had a staff of four. A woman ran the business end: selling advertising, editing, doing layout, and printing. Her son, Red, who owned a van, was in charge of distribution. An older gentleman who seemed to know everyone in town wrote the sports section, birth announcements, and obituaries. He was hired to cover everything else.

The community of twenty thousand, which was a bit too much like home, existed as a railway hub for both freight and passenger trains. It served as a transit point for freight, and as an early morning north bound, and evening south bound ride for passengers. Logging and mining surrounded the town as well. He rented a bachelor apartment above the downtown drugstore, within walking distance of the office.

As his name suggests, Red was as ginger as it gets and

freckled to match. Long and lean, he was a stringy twenty-something who loved plaid flannel shirts and galumphed around town in Kodiaks. He wasn't the brightest light, but his heart was in the right place. He lived fifteen minutes from town in a cabin with no electricity and no running water, and liked his accommodations just fine.

Every Friday morning he drove into town, loaded his van with the week's edition, and dropped off newspaper bundles at all the convenience and grocery stores in the area. Then he wrapped up the day by eating dinner and playing some pool at The Pub on Main Street. For the most part, he liked his solitude out in the bush, but he decided to take The Press' new writer under his wing in the spirit of possible friendship. Red liked the company on Friday nights and the new guy proved to be some decent competition at eight ball.

"Just part of my misspent youth at university," he explained after winning his ninth straight game with a sweet bank shot.

"Wouldn't know nothin' 'bout that. Barely graduated from high school m'self. Only got out thanks to a math teacher who never wanted to see my sorry ass again. Hey, there's someone I want you to meet." He waved to the waitress, "Hey lady, could you bring us two more beers?"

This was how he met his future wife. She was Red's cousin, a nineteen-year-old who waited tables at The Pub in the evenings while working on her Diploma of Hair and Beauty during the day.

"She's cute," he thought as she brought over their drinks. She liked him, too.

In a small community, all of the options in the dating scene are obvious and there's rarely a change in the menu. He was the new meat in town and though he wasn't grade A beef, novelty breeds curiosity. Most people who moved there didn't stay long. Those who grew up there wanted out. If they hadn't left town by the age of twenty-five they probably never would. She was determined for that not to happen to her. She liked that he was so smart and had goals. "My plan is to cut my teeth here and get some experience under my belt so I can work my way up to some big city paper, maybe even move into television. I want to get to the point where I'm writing articles and reporting on stories that make a difference, investigative journalism that holds people accountable and exposes corruption," he told her when they went out on their first date. By the end of the year, she told him, she would be a certified esthetician able to move to the city with some skills. All women want to have their hair cut and styled and their makeup done by a professional for special occasions, and she thought there were always special occasions.

    He liked her because she liked him. She liked him because he was a gentleman who might prove to be a means of getting out of the back woods. On her twentieth birthday she moved out of her mother's place and in with him. They were good together and he found doing things that made her happy gave him a unique sense of joy, something he had never experienced before. "I guess this is love," he thought.

    One night's pillow talk meandered onto the subject of kids. She wanted four or five of them someday. He'd never really considered a family. As an adult he had never been exposed to children. There were no cousins, so no family gatherings with little gaffers running around. His brother had no children, and he had no real friends who had begun the process of populating the next generation. As for children in the general public, he wasn't terribly fond of them. He didn't tell her any of this. The information might be a deal breaker, and he was enjoying having a significant other in his life. He would cross that bridge if the relationship progressed to that point.

    He just didn't expect to be crossing it so soon.

39

People are patterns. If you know anything, you know this. If you are going to have even the slightest chance of making this escape work, you have to get through the door. In order to accomplish this, you have to train your captors, lull them into a sense of habitualness so they have no expectations of anything out of the norm.

There are many ways to do this.

When Ali fought Foreman in the Rumble in the Jungle, Ali knew he couldn't beat Forman punch for punch. Foreman was too strong. The strategy was to let George to do all the punching until he had nothing left. Ali spent the first round covering up and letting Foreman whale on him with those brutal arms. When the round was over, Ali did not sit down in his corner. He remained standing, staring at Foreman to make him believe that round one was a walk in the park for Ali.

For the next few rounds, Ali just stuck to the ropes and let Foreman do his thing, but every once in a while, Ali would lean in and whisper something in George's ear. "Why you keep punching me with your right? Mustn't have much of a left." So, Foreman started throwing the left.

By the eighth round Foreman was landing punches to Ali's head, but they had no power to do any damage. And, he no longer had the strength to keep his gloves high enough to protect his own head. Ali was tired and sore but he still had his power, and when the moment came, when Foreman's hands were low, he landed four or five headshots in a row, and the fight was over. In the first few rounds, Ali essentially trained Foreman.

You know you can't fight your way out. You've never thrown a punch in your life. You have no idea what lies beyond the door, but you'll never know until you try. They unlock it when you are sleeping. This is the pattern you must exploit. You have tried feigning sleep to see when and how exactly they open the door, but you have either fallen asleep waiting or have not been convincing enough in your deception.

Repetition instills expectation. In your class, you taught your students to be quiet whenever you uttered the words, "Ladies and gentlemen." After a few repetitions of this phrase, you had them trained.

You are as strong as you are ever going to be. You are as physically rested as you have ever been. Today, you pretended to drink from your bottle of water, but you took only small sips. When almost full, the bottle is heavy and is the closest thing you have to a weapon when the time comes.

For the last two weeks, you have stuck to the same daily routine. You call it "weeks" for lack of a better term for the fourteen cycles you have endured. In particular, you have kept your sleeping ritual as consistent as possible. You fold your blanket to make a pillow and place it in almost the same spot each night, though you have been trying to creep it a little closer to the door each time. You start out on your stomach with your head towards the door and your hands by your face, then you roll over onto your side. A couple of tosses and a few turns and you end up on your back with your hands above your head. You wake up on your stomach, so you assume something causes you to roll over in your sleep.

Last night you did a successful test run. When they thought you had finally drifted off, you heard the muffled footsteps arrive, the jangle of the keychain, and the key in the lock. You felt the shift in the air as the sealed door sucked open, though you couldn't tell how wide. They must crouch low to slide your paper plate of food on the concrete then place your bottle of water on the floor. You hear someone remove your empty plate and bottle which you have learned to leave right at the threshold. The door closed, the bolt latched, the key removed, and they walked away.

You figured out what you needed to know, the one ingredient that was missing. All it took was one embarrassing memory from a warm spring morning.

40

You see, Beast was a freak of nature. If he hoped to taste vengeance, he would have to be a cunning strategist. He would have to be Ali to Beast's Foreman. He had no brawn, but did he have the brains to pull it off?

The principal of the school must have been a drill sergeant in a former life. He stood ramrod straight in front of the office each morning as the students entered. He always wore a pressed white shirt and a tie. His brush cut looked porcupine sharp. Those who had been sent to the office knew of the fountain pen. The principal took great pride in this pen as he wrote letters home to parents listing the misbehaviours of their offspring, requesting meetings to address his concerns.

He would regale each offender with the history of the pen: how it had been handed down from his grandfather to his father and finally to him, as though it were Excalibur itself. He kept it in a specially-carved wooden box on his desk. This pen was an integral part of his plan.

The schoolyard grapevine is a fascinating creature, especially in a small town. Students at first bell would know you were ill even before you did. Indeed, the grapevine was rife with unsubstantiated rumours, but it also possessed reliable information regarding the comings and goings of certain less favourable individuals who perpetrated acts of extortion, harassment, assault, and battery on many less fortunate souls attending Maple Street Public School. It was in everyone's vested interest to keep tabs on Beast and his cronies.

It was the last warm day in September, just as summer was about to turn towards fall. The forecast was for a hot and sunny afternoon, terrible weather for a math test following afternoon recess. Beast, who did not like math, had decided in the morning to instigate an evacuation into the glorious sunshine just before the test. He was planning on pulling the fire alarm during the chaos of returning from last recess. Coincidentally, the principal, who was attending a meeting elsewhere, had left the secretary in charge of the school. By lunch, the vine had spread the word, "Be ready for an early dismissal."

Opportunity was knocking. When the bell rang to summon the students back inside, they bounced through the halls in anticipation of the dive siren of the fire alarm. They were not disappointed. It sounded, as promised. Everyone exited the building into the playground, some of them leaving the property and disappearing for the day. Others stood in the sunshine with their teachers waiting for the fire trucks to arrive. By the time the "all clear" was given, only fifteen minutes remained before dismissal. The secretary decided, with the encouragement of the teachers, to keep everyone outside. Mission accomplished, in more ways than one.

The following morning, the principal marched down the hallway to Beast's classroom. In front of everyone, he was directed to empty out the contents of his desk. There, atop the pile of crumpled up paper, folded scribblers, candy bar wrappers, and other assorted odds and ends, sat Excalibur, obviously purloined during the previous day's commotion.

The principal took the theft personally. He issued a week's suspension, signed by the very pen in question, with further disciplinary action to be announced upon Beast's return to school after an extensive meeting with the parents.

Sure, he could have ratted out Beast to a teacher the previous day about the impending alarm, but his warning would have just pre-empted the crime without any consequences. He needed to take advantage of the opportunity to create an even more decisive strike.

He knew the secretary was constantly misplacing her keys. Students often saw her going from class to class asking the teachers if they had come across them. He also figured, in the evacuation, she would neglect to lock the office door. Therefore, when he came in from recess, he stationed himself just around the corner and waited. When the alarm sounded and the secretary vacated the office into the sea of children, he simply slipped in, grabbed the pen, and slipped out again. He tucked it into his sock and joined everyone outside.

After the commotion was over he went back into the school to "get his backpack" and planted the pen in the Beast's desk while no one was around. Also, on the grade four teacher's desk, he left a note which he'd written earlier in the day with his left hand to conceal his handwriting. The note simply stated who had pulled the fire alarm. The following morning, the principal did the math and connected the dots.

By October, Beast was still on the prowl for a rat. The rumour mill had not provided a name, just plenty of speculation. Most guilty people usually get caught because they can't keep their mouths shut. At some point, the need to share their accomplishments becomes overwhelming, and they let them slip. Not him. He said nothing to anyone. He played along with the theorizing of his classmates to avert any suspicion, content to keep the achievement to himself.

Yet, he was still a target because he had always *been* a target. Beast figured he hadn't punched anyone in a while and his knuckles were getting itchy. They crossed paths in the bathroom one morning.

"You're standing at my urinal."

Within seconds the conversation escalated to the "outside at lunch by the alcove" challenge. He knew that getting punched in the bathroom at that moment was pointless - no spectators - but at the noon recess, there would be a crowd of thousands after word of the showdown spread. The crowd of thousands ended up being a dozen kids including Dumb and Dumber.

The alcove was a covered fire exit away from the watchful eyes of playground supervision, an arched tunnel made of bricks and mortar. It was one of Beast's favourite places in the world. The confrontation was quick and painless, literally. Beast beat his chest and threw around derogatory epithets regarding sexual orientation, much to the crowd's amusement. As the victim-to-be, he silently stood against the inside wall.

Beast never exercised the element of surprise in a fistfight, reserving this tactic for attacks from behind trees. He loved the fact his prey knew what was coming. The fear in his victim's eyes thrilled him. He just stared at Beast and waited, refusing to show any signs of fear. The right cross came straight for his face with much force but little speed. He ducked. Beast's fist hit the bricks with a crunching sound that made the spectators cringe, then he was rolling on the ground in agony begging Dumb and Dumber to call a teacher because he thought he'd broken his hand.

This fight was the first he had ever won and he hadn't

thrown a single punch.

Finally, the week before Christmas break was the last time he'd ever have to deal with Beast's taunts and jeers. Behind his house was a hill where all the neighbourhood kids went sledding when the snow finally arrived to blanket the town. He was walking home from a Scout meeting, the frosty crystals squeaking beneath his boots with each step as a full moon illuminated the clear, cold sky. He was bundled up in a parka and had his running shoes slung over his shoulder. The shoes, brand new leather Adidas his mother had bought him the previous week, were the most expensive he had ever owned.

He was crunching his way along the hard trodden path behind the houses, heading to his back door, when he looked up the hill. His nemesis was bombing toward him on a shiny metal toboggan with Dumb and Dumber on board. He jumped out of the way just in time, avoiding having his legs taken out from under him. The toboggan skidded to a stop in a snow spray and the three stooges began circling like a wolf pack.

"Well, if it isn't our little Boy Scout. Nice kerchief. Get any faggoty badges tonight?" and Beast flicked the prized running shoes into the snow.

That was it. Those were his brand new expensive shoes and he just wasn't going to take it anymore. He deked around Beast, grabbed the toboggan, and started swinging it wildly through the air, the edge of it catching Beast in the ribs before slamming down on Dumb's back as he turtled in fear. Dumber just stood dumbstruck in petrified awe. He hurled the sled into the air. It landed almost thirty feet away. He calmly walked over to pluck his shoes from the snow, turned, and continued home as if nothing had happened. His mother met him at the back door. She had seen everything from the kitchen window while washing the dinner dishes.

"Oh my God. What did you just do?" Her eyes were wide with accusation. "You could have killed someone. What if that toboggan had hit one of them in the head? I am so disappointed in you. This is how you deal with problems, with violence? We are not going to say anything about this to your father. How could you be so irresponsible? Now, get up to your room."

The one time he actually stood up for himself and his mother was disappointed in him. He just couldn't win. At least Beast would no longer be a thorn.

41

News flash: birth control is not one hundred percent effective. There's always a slight chance of misconception. Accidents happen despite precaution. A month after her twentieth birthday, and just weeks before completing her esthetics course, her first home pregnancy test read positive; as did the second and the third. He proposed, of course. It was the responsible thing to do.

He thought an autumn wedding would give them time to make the arrangements, but she didn't want to be showing in her gown. Early July it was. The timelines were tight, but it would all work out. St. Andrew's was booked and Reverend Martin was on deck. The reception would be in the basement with music provided by some kid who owned his own sound system. The church was fine with a "wet" reception and the DJ had an older brother who would take care of the booze.

Red reluctantly agreed to be his best man. In hindsight, he should have thought better than to ask, but he didn't know the history.

The weatherman lied. It was supposed to be a sunny but cool Saturday. It wasn't. It was supposed to be one of the best days of his life, to be cherished for all time.

There was a wedding. There were flowers and presents. Relatives came in droves, as did friends and acquaintances. There was a minister and a ceremony with vows. The bride looked lovely in her flowing white gown. The bridesmaids looked less than stellar in canary yellow summer dresses. As is often the case, the style of those dresses did not suit a single body type in the group. The groomsmen were comprised of her relatives. They looked as though they had never worn formalwear before. The bride and the groom both said "I do". A young cousin sang during the signing of the official papers. They were pelted with confetti as they headed out the front door to have their photos taken.

The reception was a reception. There was food and music and wine. People made speeches. People danced. People ate and drank. At the end of the night, people went home. It had been a lovely wedding.

I just can't do it. I cannot make that day a positive one. It makes me shudder every time I think about it. Some memories can never be altered to make them more appealing. They are simply tucked away in the "it happened" file, never to be dwelled upon. The truth can cause physical discomfort.

My wife banked all her plans on it being sunny. The television weatherman confirmed a beautiful forecast the night before, but in the morning, it was overcast and drizzling.

There was no night of drinking with the boys the prior evening after the rehearsal. I had no friends to drink with other than Red, but I absolved him of the traditional responsibilities assigned to the best man other than holding on to the ring and being the official witness. He didn't even show up at the rehearsal.

We had been out playing pool when I asked him to

stand for me.

"So," I said as I racked up the next game, "it looks like I'm in need of a best man. I was wondering if you would do me the honour."

Red just stared back at me for a moment. "You serious? You want me to be your best man?"

"You're my best friend," I told him. That was a stretch. Other than playing pool together one night a week for the last few months, we never hung out together. Our conversations were mostly work related or small town gossip, nothing constituting a deep friendship. Still, he was the closest thing I had.

"You sure you don't have an old university buddy you can call up and ask?"

"Can't say there was a lot of bonding happening with me in university. Look, if you don't want to I could probably ask…"

"Nah. It's OK. If you want me to, I will. What do you need me to do?"

"Nothing really. Just be there on the wedding day."

"I guess I can do it. Do I need to buy a suit?"

"We're renting tuxes. I'll pay for yours if you…"

"Nah. It's OK. I'll cover it."

However, I sensed that something was not right. There was an odd look in his eye. For the rest of the evening he no longer seemed present. He drank a bit more than usual and he certainly wasn't paying much attention to the pool table, missing shots he could usually make with his eyes closed.

When Red showed up half an hour before the ceremony, he was weaving down the aisle. He looked like shit in spite of the tux. His hair was a mess, he hadn't shaved, and his eyes were half closed with alcohol.

"I'll be fine," he slurred. "Just tell me where to stand."

The minister pulled me aside and explained that he

would not allow Red to be an official witness, not in his condition. I convinced the padre to allow Red to stand with me, but I would ask my father to sign the register.

I'm just glad my bride didn't see him before the service; she had enough on her plate to deal with.

As the ceremony was about to begin, I realized that Red had disappeared with the ring in his pocket. He could not be located anywhere. No one bothered to check the church nursery where he had found a comfortable mat to pass out on. My father stepped in and my mother loaned me her ring so the ceremony could proceed.

As my bride proceeded down the aisle, Red's absence and my father's presence at the front of the church showed in the whites of her eyes. No one had told her the best man was AWOL. As she joined me, I leaned in and whispered that everything was going to be fine. She was none too pleased when my mother's ring would not fit on her finger.

While we were signing the register, my wife's ten-year-old cousin sat at the piano to sing and play what was supposed to be a cute and touching rendition of "Can You Feel the Love Tonight". But stage fright got the best of him as he headed into the first chorus and his fingers fumbled on the keys. He panicked and lost track of where he was. He tried starting over again but was unable to pull it together, crying in frustration. His mother had to escort him back to their pew to console him.

Had I been a guest, the events of the day would have been kind of funny, but I was the groom whose bride had planned for her perfect day. One person's tragedy is another person's comedy.

The drizzle had abated when we stepped outside of the church with confetti in our hair. The women's heals sank into the soggy ground. We drove to the river for photographs. A picturesque peninsula jutted out into the water's flow. We parked the vehicles in the public lot off of Oak Street and trekked down a one-hundred-yard dirt path. The photographer tried to find the positives in the weather, saying that direct sunlight is actually too harsh and the cloud cover worked in our favour. Part of their job is to find silver linings.

We managed to get a few shots of the entire wedding party before a large clap of thunder opened up the sky. The torrential rain was joined by a sudden strong wind from the north. By the time we reached the cars, we were soaked to the skin, and several members of the wedding party were covered in mud, having tripped and fallen in the chaos. We returned to the reception looking like a pack of wet dogs. My wife's dress was the proverbial cake that someone left out in the rain.

There is no wedding picture on our mantle.

We dried off but spent the rest of the evening in uncomfortable, itchy, damp clothes.

The ladies of the church prepared the meal of dry chicken, cold potatoes, and soggy vegetables.

I'd like to say it's a good thing the DJ's brother was over-pouring the shots at the open bar, but the booze became another complication later in the evening.

After the overly mixed bass woke him up, Red finally made his appearance as the music began. He skulked into the reception and he pulled me aside, apologizing all over himself. He was still feeling the fumes. When I asked him for the ring so I could make the swap, he fumbled around in all of his pockets, searched the nursery, and tried to retrace his foggy steps. It was no use. The ring was gone. My wife threw eye-daggers at him. Red headed to the bar to drown his incompetence and whatever demons were haunting him.

Open bars are dangerous creatures. Fortunately, my wife's uncle was paying for the alcohol. An open bar results in people not being as possessive of their beverages: they get up to dance, and forget where they left their glass. So, they return to the bar to get another.

My fourteen-year-old brother took advantage of the situation. I had asked my parents to keep a watchful eye on him, but what could they do with a teenage son at a wedding, force him to remain seated at the table? Junior worked the perimeter of the hall and whenever someone got up to dance, he nabbed the unattended booze and pounded it back unnoticed. I caught him doing it from across the room and shot him a glare. He threw me the finger with a grin on his face.

An hour later I saw him slinking off with some older teenage girl. He looked more seasoned than his fourteen years and had the thick long rocker hair and broody appearance the girls loved. I followed, but lost them in a long hallway that led to the bathrooms. When I finally stumbled across them in an alcove off the sanctuary, his hand was up her dress and hers was down his pants.

"Come on, bro," he said as I shooed his conquest away, "You shouldn't be the only one getting lucky tonight."

I angrily reminded him of the inappropriateness of his actions, especially in a church.

He just smiled and said, "It was going to be righteous."

I dragged him back to the reception and said nothing to my parents. Why ruin their evening?

Over by the bar, Red was having a very hushed and somber conversation with a lanky brunette in a sky blue dress. Many of the guests were paying close attention with concerned looks on their faces. One of the guests told me that the woman was there with her new boyfriend.

"And that is significant because…?" I asked.

"Oh, don't you know? She and Red were engaged last year. She left him standing at the altar in this very church and ran off with the other guy. Didn't your wife tell you? Red's ex is her second cousin." Some missing pieces of a complicated puzzle had just fallen into place. As the image started to form in my mind, the boyfriend decided to step in.

"Look, pal. Why don't you just leave her alone? She's done with you," at which point he placed a hand on Red's chest and proceeded to push him away. Not a good idea.

Suddenly, both men were rolling around on the floor trying to fit in punches whenever one of them ended up on top. The crazy thing was no one stepped in to stop them. Some of the locals were actually cheering Red on. If he hadn't been so inebriated, Red could have taken him, but his flailing fists were missing their mark. When it became obvious that Red was about to have his ass handed to him, a couple of guys from the pool hall stepped in to pull the boyfriend off. All the while, my wife just stood there, drop-jawed, with tears welling up in her eyes. There was still more to come.

My parents had been watching the tableau of events from their table all evening. This was not exactly what they expected of their son's wedding, but they smiled politely and had cordial conversations with other guests who became progressively sloppy with alcohol over the course of the night.

Junior continued his clandestine theft of drinks and was certainly feeling no pain as he accompanied my parents to the door where my new bride and I were saying goodbye to the guests as they departed.

Both parents gave my wife a hug and told her what a lovely day it had been. Just as Junior reached out to shake her hand, the accumulation of pilfered cocktails rose to the surface and he threw up all over the front of her dress. Outside, the rain continued to pour.

Was our wedding really that disastrous? Has time caused my memory to fester, making the day worse than it really was? Red really did lose the ring and disappeared before the ceremony. There *was* a physical altercation between him and his ex's current boyfriend. We did get rained on while posing for photos. There is no wedding picture of my wife and me. The food was terrible and there was, indeed, a lot of drinking. Especially by Junior - he did puke all over my wife. I do remember that vividly, but I'm not positive about all the rest.

Have I just amped up all of the details? Why would I do that? Maybe to foreshadow, in retrospect, the less than satisfactory married life I embarked upon.

I should have seen it coming.

42

" ... that he rose again the third day according to the scriptures." 1 Corinthians 15:4. Easter Sunday was unusually warm that April. Spring had come early, the world was budding and blossoming, and the family decided to walk to church. The minister greeted them at the door as they came in out of the morning warmth and sun. Tension remained in their respective smiles, despite the months since their confrontational dinner. Today would not help to improve the relationship.

The two older girls headed off to don their choir gowns while he and his wife made their way up the stairs with their youngest to the second-floor balcony overlooking the sanctuary of polished wood and burgundy carpets. They sat in the same place every Sunday, an informal claim of territory. From above, they had an open view of the service. The pulpit was adorned in springtime flowers and purple parament to celebrate the liturgical season. The sun shining through the rich colours of stained glass windows dappled the pews in multi-coloured splendor. Though he was not much for the spirituality, he did appreciate the architecture and peaceful ambiance of old churches.

He always made good use of this hour each Sunday when the world slowed down to reflect upon more important matters requiring his personal attention, tuning out the rote formulaic rituals around him. He often found himself lost in his own thoughts, being drawn back to reality each time the extensive pipes of the organ signalled the beginning of another hymn.

After the junior choir sang, the older girls joined them in the balcony.

The theme of the morning's service was: looking for the signs of God's love. There were scripture readings supporting the concept of how God reveals himself to mankind through nature, conscience, the Bible, and, of course, through Jesus Christ. When it came time for the sermon, the minister stood behind the pulpit. As always, his voice shifted even more deeply into his solemn ethereal tone. "He is risen," he began. "Hallelujah, He is risen."

Heat rises and the church balcony was awash in the warmth of the morning sun. It was at this point that he usually allowed his own thoughts to tune out the preacher's voice. That particular morning, the combination of the warmth of the sunshine, the aroma of candle wax, and the drone of the minister's breathy, otherworldly voice lulled him. He caught himself nap-jerking a couple of times. He shifted in his pew while he stifled a yawn. Ten minutes in, he could resist no longer and his head began to loll backward.

"Saturday evening, when the Sabbath ended," the minister quoted from scripture, "Mary Magdalene, Mary the mother of James, and Salome went out and purchased burial spices so they could anoint Jesus' body. Very early on Sunday morning, just at sunrise, they went to the tomb. On the way they were asking each other, 'Who will roll away the stone for us from the entrance to the tomb?' But as they arrived, they looked up and saw that the stone, which was very large, had already been rolled aside."

At this particular moment, with his head tipped back and his mouth agape in slumber, he emitted, from the back of his arid, closing throat, a resonant snore, much like a diesel engine sparking to life, which reverberated throughout the sanctuary. He startled himself awake and in the brief moment of his own confusion blurted out the first word that came to mind: "Amen," he said in a booming voice.

All eyes turned toward him. The older, more reverent members of the congregation glared in disdain. Some suppressed their laughter. The children began to giggle. The minister slowly shook his head. His wife elbowed him in the ribs, blushing with embarrassment.

43

Why did your fake slumber fool them last night? Because you knew they were listening and remembered the one element you had neglected to incorporate before: you snore.

The difficulty in pretending to snore is that you don't really know what you sound like unless someone makes an audio recording when you are in full blow, but no one's ever done that. Your wife imitated the sound on many occasions, but you figured she was exaggerating to make a point. Lord knows it certainly became a bone of contention in your marriage.

It's a good thing your mind wandered through the church doors to that warm spring morning's sermon, or you might never have figured it out.

44

I would like to think the toboggan incident was my coup de grace with Beast. I had finally stood my ground and fought back. It was Independence Day no matter what my mother thought. It's true, I never had to deal with his harassing comments or physical assaults ever again.

That Christmas break, Beast disappeared from my life once and for all, quite literally. When classes resumed in January, there was an obvious absence in the hallowed halls of education. Beast was gone. He was still in town, so to speak, but had been admitted to hospital with a broken arm and ribs, multiple contusions to his face, and a ruptured spleen. No, not from the toboggan.

Apparently, on New Year's Eve, his father had gone on a bender. This was not unusual. Everyone in town knew he was a drunk, but no one really grasped how mean a drunk he had been to his family behind closed doors. He had been at one of the local bars, ushering in the New Year. When the owner told him he'd had enough and asked him to leave, he became belligerent with a few of the other patrons. He refused when asked politely, so the bouncers stepped in and weren't as civil.

He stumbled home madder than hell. The walk in the cold did nothing to cool his temper and when he arrived home, he decided his wife should become the target of his hostilities. The snide comments about her appearance grew into a barrage of insults about her inabilities and shortcomings as a wife and mother. When she started to cry, he yelled at her to suck it up and get her shit together. He was tired of her whimpering and whining all the time. When her tears wouldn't stop he lashed out with the back of his hand across her face. His rage took over and when she hit the floor he proceeded to kick at her in his stupor.

Beast had been in his bedroom listening to music. He'd become accustomed to the yelling over the years and to the occasional slap, but when he heard the sound of kicking and stomping coming from the living room, he rushed in to defend his mother. He barrelled into the room and tackled his father in the chest with his full weight, leaving them both on the floor. The father was winded and Beast didn't know what to do next. He got to his feet and started yelling at his father to calm the fuck down or he would call the police. The father rose from the floor with the devil in his eye and was fixed on the young man standing in front him. Beast was fine in a fight with those who were smaller than he was, but nothing had prepared him for the fury of a grown man whose senses had been diluted by alcohol.

The mother stood in horror as the father unleashed on the boy with fists and elbows, knees and boots. He would have killed him had the mother not seen the hockey stick propped by the front door. She retrieved it and started swinging it wildly at the father. The blade caught him in the ear. When he hunched over in pain, she swung low and took out his left knee, separating the joint. With the father rolling around on the floor in the throes of agony, she called the police. The father was arrested and Beast was taken to Emergency, and admitted to the hospital.

The town was abuzz with the story, many of the specifics provided by one of the officers who showed up on the scene. He had shared with his wife some of the details from the official report, making her a sought-after fount of information for the rumour mill during the next few weeks.

When Beast was finally released, the mother packed up the house, filed for divorce, and left town for parts unknown with her son by her side.

I have never told anyone the real reason why Beast no longer tormented me. It's always better to let them believe that when I stood up for myself he finally backed down. No sense in spoiling such an inspirational tale with something as insignificant as the truth.

45

Everyone experiences selective blindness. There are things in the past everyone chooses not to see. With repetition, the blindness becomes the norm. The brain is trained to ignorance, obliviousness.

He is no different.

"Irish" worked as an editor in the non-fiction department at the publishing house. Because she had a Celtic first name that everyone either misspelled or mispronounced, she nipped the problem in the bud by always introducing herself with, "...but you can call me Irish." She spoke with a hint of the brogue passed on by her parents. He enjoyed listening to her speak at meetings. The songfullness tickled his ear and made him grin. She was in her mid-to-late twenties and married to a travelling salesman who was rarely home. What he sold was unknown. She had never mentioned; he had never overheard. They had never had a personal conversation. What he knew about her came from eavesdropping in the lunchroom and from the gossipy conversations floating through the air around him.

He surmised things were not good in her marriage, that

she suspected not all of her husband's travel was work-related. He caught snippets of conversations when, staving off tears over a cup of tea, she confided her suspicions to co-workers who had become friends.

His perfect smile radiated through the pebbled, non-reflective glass of the framed photograph on her desk. He had great hair, a strong jaw, broad shoulders, with eyes glinting of charm and mischief. It was easy to see why he caught the attention of other women, even in a photo.

It was a decent company Christmas party, as far as Christmas parties go. Smyth had arranged for an exceptional caterer and a well-stocked bar. It was obvious that profits had been strong that year and rumours of bonuses were circulating.

The boardroom had been decked out as party central but the festivities spread throughout the bullpen, a sea of cubicles where most of the staff worked in open isolation.

He found himself in the Marketing Department with a plate of nibblies in one hand and a mug of spiked eggnog in the other. A cluster of employees were laughing and telling tales as they shared in the Christmas cheer. Irish was sitting in the thick of it. She had an infectious laugh and had lost herself in the warmth of the rum and the peacock stories of the young movers and shakers. He stood on the periphery, leaning over one of the half walls.

"Hey there," one of the millennial marketing gurus said, drawing him into the conversation. "Got any of your stories from the good old days of the newspaper business?" There was a hint of condescension in his tone.

He knew he was a bit of a dinosaur in this particular crowd and the "good old days" comment made him feel his age; yet he was never one to turn down an opportunity to share an anecdote or two from his time as a reporter with the local paper. He took the spotlight and for the next half hour had them enthralled, and at times in stitches, with the back-stories and transgressions of some of the more infamous members of town council. He could certainly spin a good yarn. He also had sharp instincts about when to quit. He wrapped up the show on a high note before passing the torch to another in huddle then started to make his way back to the boardroom when some guy from accounting caught up to him.

"Hey, Buddy. Good stuff back there. You've really had an interesting life."

"It's not over yet, I hope. Still got some good years left in me."

"Touché. I'm just surprised you walked away."

He was confused. "Walked away from what?"

"You're kiddin', right? You didn't see the way Irish was into you?"

The remark caught him off-guard. He truly hadn't noticed. "What do you mean?"

"Oh, Dude, she had eyes for ya, believe me. You really didn't notice?"

He felt foolish. He was so unaccustomed to anyone ever flirting with him that he wouldn't know the signs if they slapped him across the face. "Oh, I think you're reading more into it than there is. She was just enjoying herself, I'm sure."

"If she'd have been lookin' at me that way, I'd be workin' out an exit plan to ditch with her."

He was flushed with the thought. "Well, we're both married and you know what they say about relationships in the workplace."

"Suit yourself, but I bet she'll be seeking you out later."

She *had* been listening very intently to his stories, now that he thought about it. She had also casually touched his arm a couple of times in the midst of her laughter. "Maybe Buddy was right," he thought. He felt flattered, though he questioned the veracity of the young man's remarks. He had long ago accepted his generally dumpy appearance and abrasive personality and thought that anyone so attractive having any interest in him was unlikely. However, the concept was a pleasant possibility.

Not half an hour later, she was standing next to him within another circle of revellers by the dessert table. He was more aware of her this time. She brushed up against his shoulder, making the hair stand up on the back of his neck. There was plenty of space, yet she was incredibly close to him. He couldn't help but admire her figure. She reminded him of golden age movie starlets, when curves were still appreciated. Whenever they made eye contact, her smile warmed to his gaze.

He never would have noticed. He had become so numb to the possibility of physical attention and attraction from another human being over the years of his marriage, he was blind to the signals. He felt a bit giddy, not that he would pursue it. Just the idea of the possibility was enough. "But what if?" he thought. "Just once?" He tried to push the enticement from his mind. He was the responsible one, after all.

Just then Buddy broke his reverie, "tell 'em the one about the speeding ticket you got."

The distraction was nice while it lasted. It would be savoured again in the weeks to come.

46

In *Inferno*, the first of three sections of *The Divine Comedy* by Danté Alighieri, Danté and Virgil travel down through the rings of hell in search of the divine. They reach the eighth ring, designated for the fraudsters. There are numerous layers or pouches of fraud.

The twenty-first and twenty-second cantos describe the fifth layer: grafting, accepting money for political favour. These sinners spend eternity in a vat of boiling pitch, a horrific form of eternal suffering. Some of them seek temporary relief from the excruciating pain by extending their limbs or arching their backs out of the pitch like frogs or turtles, but when they do, they are plucked from the tar by winged demons who torture them in more terrible ways before throwing them back in. The sinners come to realize that being in the pitch is a better alternative to the unknown forms of cruelty they will suffer at the hands of the demons. It is the hell they know.

Inferno kept popping up in my studies at university. It is the go-to allegorical text for literature, philosophy, art, and, of course, religion. Now I find myself held captive in this cell of darkness, another form of pitch. It has become the hell I know.

Yet, here I am, planning an escape, not knowing what demons might be lurking outside that door or what fate awaits me if I fail.

Am I a fraud as well, destined to spend eternity in the pitch? Should I simply accept my circumstances and wait for what feels like an eternity for my freedom, or take the risk? I've never been the risk taker. I've always chosen the safest course. It was always the responsible thing to do.

To hell with responsible.

47

March is such a nondescript month. It is winter, but not. It is spring, but not. It is dirty snow and slush with freezing rain and grey skies. It is the month without hope: the hope has been destroyed by February's bleakness, with April still too far away.

He was driving through the sloppy streets toward his father's nursing home with the grey weight upon his shoulders. He felt the heaviness of the transitional season and the accumulation of responsibilities accompanying each new day. He played chauffeur every weekday morning, dropping off each daughter at a different school, then picking up his mother and driving her to spend the day with his father, and finally getting himself to work. After work he reclaimed his mother and returned her to her apartment before heading home for dinner. Nights when he taught, his mother travelled by bus.

He had decided that the financial benefits of owning one vehicle usually outweighed the inconvenience. His wife was responsible for driving the kids to their evening activities, but he would often have to fill in for her if her day was plagued by personal issues. If additional rides were necessary, the parents of the girls' friends drove them home after extracurricular activities.

He was looking forward to warmer, snow-free weather when the option of riding his bike two days a week saved him from his daily route about town. He parked his car, and bracing himself against the frigid air cutting through his winter coat, crossed the open expanse to the entrance. The desk supervisor buzzed him into the secure facility without even looking up from the book he was reading. He rode the elevator to the fifth floor and walked the gloomy halls to his father's room.

As he approached, he heard an odd sound emanating from beyond the doorway. Laughter. His father was chuckling in a tired, gravelly voice. It was accompanied by the familiar voice of another.

"Well, look what the cat dragged in," he said as he crossed the threshold into the room. Junior was sitting in the chair next to his father's bed. His mother was nowhere to be seen. They had not seen each other or spoken in over three years. Junior rose from the chair and turned, extending a hand. "Good to see ya, Bro." The handshake was tenuous.

"Not off cruising the seven seas?"

"Ended our contract early. One of the guys just wasn't feelin' it anymore, so we all decided to cut it short, go home, and regroup. I'd forgotten what winter was like around here."

From what he had been able to glean from his mother, Junior's life was transient, putting together bands and negotiating contracts with cruise lines to provide entertainment in the many shipboard bars. He hadn't seen winter since he turned twenty.

"Where's Mom?"

"Told her to take the afternoon off and go do something for herself like grab a cappuccino, hang out at the library."

"When did you get back?"

"Coupla weeks ago. Just got all settled in and thought I should come and see how Mum and Dad were doin'."

"That's nice of you." He felt his jaw tightening.

"Was just telling Dad some of my adventures as a pirate of the Caribbean."

"A what?"

"The name of our band: *Pirates of the Caribbean*. I know. Cheesy as hell, but they lap up that shit."

"Please tell me you don't dress the part."

"The bass player has an eye-patch. He's the one who ditched. But, nah, we don't go that far."

Neither one knew where to take the conversation next.

"Well," came a voice from the bed, "don't just stand there gawking at each other. Grab a chair."

He went around the curtain, nabbed one from the groaning neighbour's side of the room, and placed it at the foot of his father's bed. "So, Dad, it must be good to see Junior again," he said, taking a seat.

"Has he been away?"

"Just a few days, Dad," Junior jumped in. "Not long." He turned to his brother. "By the way, Mum's the only one who calls me Junior anymore. I go by J.R. now. Dad doesn't even remember my name. Kinda funny when you think about it."

"Not really." They looked at each other. "He doesn't remember mine, either."

Junior had certainly grown up. His hair was still long, but wasn't hanging over his eyes. He had it pulled back into some silly-looking bun. His beard was trimmed to his face, unlike the unkempt, hippy look he was sporting the last time they had seen each other. However, he still had that crazy gleam in his eye.

"Hey, Dad. Do you like having both your sons in the same room at the same time?" J.R. asked.

"Oil and pepper," his father chuckled.

"Oil and water, Dad. It's oil and water," the older son corrected.

"Oil and pepper's fine, too. One floats on the top while the other sinks to the bottom, unless of course you stir it all up," J.R. said with a grin.

"Which one of us is the pepper?"

"Oh, definitely you, Bro. I always sink to the bottom." They held each other's eyes for an awkward moment.

Their father was propped up in his bed, staring at his hands. "You two never get along. Just like last summer at Crystal Lake in the canoe."

He looked at his father. "Dad, we've never been to Crystal Lake. That's where you used to go with *your* father when *you* were a kid. Junior and I have never been in a canoe together."

"Oh, sure we have," J.R. chimed in. "Just last year. Remember, Bro? You were in the back and I was in the front and at the end of every stroke I'd accidentally splash you with water. You got so fed up with me you dunked the whole canoe. I remember, Dad."

He leaned in to his brother and whispered, "What the hell are you talking about?"

"Just go with it," he replied. "Then what happened, Dad?"

"Oh, you... you weren't wearing a..."

"Life jacket?"

"Right. Life jacket. You couldn't swim and you went under. I had to dive under to pull you up before you drowned. When we got to shore, you smacked me upside the head for almost killin' ya."

"Well," J.R. laughed, it was *your* damn fault."

Their father nodded his head and smiled into his open

hands.

Again, he leaned over and said to his brother, "That makes no sense at all. I thought I was the one who dunked the boat, not him."

"It's a story from when he was a kid. He dunked the canoe and almost drowned another kid. He just thinks it was you and me, kinda."

"Dad, that happened when you were a kid…"

"Just leave it," J.R. cut him off, rolling his eyes.

"But he's wrong. How's he going to keep things straight if we don't…"

"Keep things straight? What's the point? Do you think he's gonna get better?"

"Well, no. It's just…"

"Then have some fun and just play along."

"How can I play along when I have no idea what he's talking about? All his memories are messed up and make no sense."

"For Christ's sake, you're the writer, aren't you? Look, there's this improv kinda game we used to play in school. No matter what the other person says, just say 'yes, and…' and let them keep going. All correcting him does is piss him off."

So, they spent the next hour letting their father stumble through fragmented meandering stories pieced together from the shards of his memory. His father was doing something he hadn't seen him do in months. He was smiling. It was nice to see.

Junior had a gift with most people. No matter how annoyed he made them - his friends, his teachers, his parents - he would always do or say something that would elicit a smile, taking the edge off some of the most stressful circumstances. The charm worked on everyone but him. Nothing Junior ever had ever done had made him smile - except for the time he got suspended for telling that son-of-a-bitch teacher to go fuck himself in front of the whole class.

One of the nursing staff brought in the dinner which his mother usually fed to her husband before heading home for the evening. J.R. took the tray, pulled the rolling table over, and sat on the edge of the bed. He tied a bib around his father's neck and proceeded to spoon food into his father's mouth, reminding him to chew and swallow with each bite. J.R. was a patient man with his Dad and took great care in the task, keeping his father's face free of anything that dribbled from the sides of his mouth. He watched his brother and father in silence.

"Not that this crap gave me an appetite," J.R. said, gesturing with the spoon to the now empty tray, "but I haven't eaten since breakfast. Wanna go grab a bite somewhere? Maybe have a coupla beers?"

"Um, OK." This was new territory for them. "I'll just call home and let them know."

They ended up at a pub a few blocks away. The brothers sat in a dingy booth in the back corner.

"So," trying to make conversation, "where are you staying?"

"On Mum's couch."

"I figured that. I mean in the city. You're gone for half a year at a time. Surely you don't pay rent on a place when you're gone."

"I don't pay rent," J.R. said, shaking his head. "I own my own place."

"You own...? How can you afford that?" He caught himself. "Did Mom and Dad help you out?"

This time it was J.R.'s jaw that began to tighten. "Mum and Dad don't need to help me out, thanks. I do just fine on my own."

"How could you possibly afford a house in the city, what with the market these days?"

J.R. took a deep breath. He could feel his blood pressure start to rise. "If you really need to know, it's a three-storey house. It was in rough shape when I picked it up for significantly less than the asking price. It had been sitting there for over a year without an offer. I live on the ground floor and have the basement for a rehearsal space. There's three one-bedroom apartments on the second and third floors. I rent them out to students or other musicians. When I'm not in town, a buddy rents the basement from me for his band to practise. All the rentals cover my mortgage and taxes."

"You said it was in rough shape when you picked it up. Did Mom and Dad pay for the repairs?"

"What's with the whole 'Mum and Dad' and 'money' thing? It's my house. I paid for it and I took care of the renovations myself. Actually, that's only half-true. A couple of musician buddies of mine are contractors by day. They did the big stuff and in exchange I did a bunch of session work for them for free. The rest of the stuff I did myself. Dad taught *me* how to work with tools, too." There was a definite bite to his words.

"What's your problem? I was just asking."

J.R. wanted to go off on him, but thought better of it. "Fine," he said. "Let's get some food." He waved the waitress over and they placed their order.

The waitress was being more than friendly with J.R. "Nothing changes," he thought. They sat in silence waiting for their meals to arrive, sipping on their drinks and passively watching a soccer game on one of the big screens close by.

The accusation seemed to come from out of nowhere. "You really don't like me, do you?" J.R. had just finished his beer and leaned back, sprawling out over the booth bench.

"Why is that?"

"I like you just fine," he replied but his tone wasn't terribly convincing.

"Bullshit. You always look down your nose at me. I've never been good enough to be *your* brother, have I?"

"I just don't get you is all."

"Why? Because I didn't follow in your footsteps?"

"There's no way you ever could."

"Ooo. Ouch. There you go, lifting yourself up while putting me down. You don't even realize you're doin' it. How the hell could I ever live up to you? You were the golden child. The sun shone out of your ass."

"Oh, give me a break. No one paid any attention to me; they were always too busy dealing with you and all of your shit."

"My shit? Look, I get it, I was a pretty challenging kid, but everything just moved too fast for me. Nothing made sense. Was that my fault? Nope. It just was what it was and I did my best to figure it out. But that's kinda hard to do when everyone's always sayin' 'why can't you be more like your older brother?' It's all I ever heard at school. Everything always came so friggin' easy for you."

"Easy. You think it's all been so easy? I was dealing with my own crap the whole time you were growing up but I had no one to turn to 'cause Mom and Dad had enough on their plate and had no time for me. I had to figure it out all on my own."

"Again, you think that's my fault?"

"It has nothing to do with fault. You existed," he blurted out without thinking. He saw the look in J.R.'s eyes. He couldn't take the remark back so he decided to keep going forward. "Now look at you, traipsing around the world, working on cruise ships of all things. You call yourself a musician. You just play drums. You hit things. What kind of life is that? No direction. No future."

"Who the fuck..."

"You're certainly not around to help out with Mom and Dad now that they could really use an extra hand. It all falls on me because you're too self-absorbed to care about what happens to anybody else, especially your family."

"Really. Who just couldn't wait to get out of the house and out of town as fast as he could? That's you, *brother*. You got out and never looked back. You hardly ever came home. I might as well have been an only child. At least then I wouldn't have had to live in your fuckin' shadow, and as for my life, who are you to judge? My life is just fine, thank you very much. Just 'cause it doesn't fit your mould... You're right. I don't have a typical boring existence like most people, like you. I chose a lifestyle over a career and it's just fine with me. I couldn't live in your shoes. I'd die of boredom."

Just then the waitress arrived with their food and placed it on the table. J.R. watched her walk away, then took some money from his wallet. "I've lost my appetite," he said as he tossed the cash on the table. "Dinner's on me," and he left.

This had been their first argument as adults. It wouldn't be their last.

48

It's now or never. You have followed your routine and it's time to put your plan into action. You can't help but feel the anticipation manifesting in your gut. The small knot has been developing throughout the day and continues to worsen as you lie down with your head on the blanket, your almost full bottle of water close at hand. There are so many unknowns even if you get through the door. Which direction should you go? Will there be only one person to stand in your way? Will you find other locked doors as impassible obstacles? You just don't know.

You try to relax, to calm down. Deep cleansing breaths, over and over to slow your heart rate, only serve to make your mouth dry. You will your body to melt into the floor. You have to stay loose. Lying on your stomach is more uncomfortable now, what with the nervousness focusing itself just above your navel. Your palms are sweaty. "Stick to the plan." You roll onto your right side just like you always do. You count Mississippis, then roll over onto your left. You force yourself to think of other things, to not dwell on the possibility of failure and its consequences. But your thoughts keep circling back.

They have not caused you any harm so far. You have not been tortured or abused in any literal sense. You have remained compliant in self-preservation, but you are about to alter the status quo. Will things change for the worse if you're caught? Probably. You can't think about it. You must succeed. It's a risk you have to take, you are obligated to take. It is the duty of a prisoner to escape, isn't it? That's what you've read, what you've seen in the movies.

Over onto your back you go, just like every night, your hands stretched out above your head. Nine hundred Mississippis until you should be in fake slumber. You concentrate on the numbers. They keep you focused. You deepen your breathing and relax the back of you throat, permitting the incoming air to blend between your mouth and your nose. Your breathing becomes raspy and ragged. Your breaths grow longer and deeper. Any time now…

Long minutes pass…

Finally, a sound from beyond the door: muffled steps approaching. Your heart is racing. "Calm down," you keep reminding yourself. The jingle of the keys as one of them slides into the lock. You are waiting for the moment when the suction of air tells you the door seal has broken. "This isn't going to work!" runs through your head again and again.

The door opens. The air shifts. "Now," you tell yourself. Nothing. Your body won't move. You hear the paper plate scrape across the floor. Hands feel around for your empty water bottle, but it's not there. "Do it, now," you silently scream at yourself. Still nothing.

The door closes. The bolt is thrown. The lock is reset. The key is withdrawn and the footsteps move away from the door. The moment is lost. "Coward."

The next night. You will not chicken out. You just overwhelmed yourself yesterday. That's all. Cold feet. It won't happen again. You repeat the process. You're on your back, throat relaxed. You wait.

Footsteps. Keys. The change in air pressure. You roll onto your front and push up hard from the ground holding the water bottle in your hand. You plow into the door with your shoulder and feel the resistance of the body weight behind it. You hear someone topple. Ducking low, you clear the door-sill and turn left. Whoever is on the floor grunts while they struggle to their feet.

Everything is still black. You can't see. You are trying to move quickly through the darkness but you must remain cautious to avoid running into anything. Your left hand is on the wall, steering you as you move forward.

Suddenly, you are grabbed from behind by the shoulder. Strong fingers curl around the fabric of your sack cloth shirt. You react, spinning quickly, the bottle of water picking up centrifugal force as it arcs through the air. It connects with the side of their face, at least that's what it sounds like. They crumple to the floor. You're surprised. It actually worked.

You continue down the hallway using the wall as your guide. Twenty feet. Thirty feet.

It's as far as you get.

49

There's what I know, what I think I know, what I'm not sure I know, what I don't know, and what I've totally made up. I know that I hit Beast with a sled. I have absolutely no memory of the attack, but my mother watched me through the window.

What I remember is having my shoes flicked into the snow. Then there's a brief hiccough in time, followed by my retrieving my shoes from the snow and walking home wondering why Beast and Dumb were curled up on the ground groaning. The only explanation I have is that I became so filled with rage that I blacked out. I truly have no memory of doing the damage my mother claims I did.

Here's what I think I know. I think Beast punched the wall. It's the only sensible explanation because the following week, he was wearing a cast. I'm not sure though. I don't really remember ducking or hearing the crunch of bone. That scenario has been fabricated to fill the hole. I really don't remember. I could have pissed my pants, but no one would have let me live that down. A teacher could have intervened and sent us all on our merry way, but that doesn't ring true either. I think he punched the wall. I would have been bent over, huddling in fear. I'm not even sure if Beast and his buddies threw me in the lake or not. I ended up in the lake, but I might have fallen in when retrieving my broken bike.

And then there's what I've made up. Beast did, indeed, get caught with Excalibur in his desk the day after pulling the fire alarm. That is because *he* is the one who stole it. It was *his* plan to sneak into the office, not mine. He was caught because a note had been left on the grade four teacher's desk. The note was probably written by a student in grade four who anonymously reported it to the authorities. I just *wanted* to be the one. I wanted to be smarter, cunning enough to pull something like that off. I never had the chance for revenge, because when I actually did fight back with the toboggan, this winter scene was never sketched upon the panel of my memory.

The real kicker is that, every once in a while, I actually believe I was responsible for his getting caught.

How fucked is that?

50

Death has received mixed reviews, mostly negative ones, but there are times when it's a blessing, a bittersweet gift.

During the summer months his father withdrew even farther from the world, his mind losing its brilliant treasure trove of information, his memories sinking into an abyss. The son's heartbroken imagination watched as the once-brilliant colours on the brain's palette began merging into black... fading into grey... bleaching into white... and... disappearing... into... oblivion. What remained was a glassy, vacant stare, lacking of recognition, an occasional nod of feigned affirmation, and an absence of verbal communication. As he no longer remembered how to swallow, feeding him had become impossible.

Just after his father had been institutionalized, he sat down with his mother one afternoon over coffee and had the inevitable pragmatic discussion about death and the arrangements that had been prepared well in advance. She informed him everything had already been paid for and planned out: cremation, burial plot, selection of urns, composition of epitaphs.

"There were so many details left unattended to when your grandfather passed. We promised ourselves not to burden our own children with all of it," she proudly explained. "As for our wills," she continued, "they are fairly straightforward." She pulled a manila envelope from her bag and handed it to him. "Here's your copy. Dad and I have made you executor, if that's all right with you."

Of course it was. Who else would they choose?

"After we're both gone, our property should be sold off and added to the overall estate, which is to be divided equally between you and your brother."

He looked through the contents of the envelope and came across a financial statement of his parents' current net worth. It was substantial without being obscene. They had obviously managed their investments well over the years.

"Equally?" he asked, a look of concern on his face.

"Yes, equally. Why would you think otherwise?"

"Mom, no offence, but is that wise? Junior is - how shall I put it - impulsive. He wouldn't know how to deal with such a – with this much money. He also doesn't have any children, any family, to support."

"I appreciate your concerns," she said, holding up her hand to stop him from saying any more. She was expecting his resistance. "Your father and I decided it is the only fair solution. Yes, you have three children and he has none..."

"That we know of."

"...but you have a stable career and are probably much better off than he is. It will help him remain on a firm footing."

"If he doesn't just piss it away."

"Well, that will be his choice to make. He's an adult and he seems to be doing fine lately."

He knew her decision was final.

"Besides," she tried to lighten the mood, "your father

might not be doing very well right now, but I intend to be around for quite a while yet."

"Sorry, Mom. I was just..." There was nothing more to be said.

By the end of October, his father had slipped into unconsciousness and was being sustained through an I.V. tube. He was still breathing on his own, but experienced no signs of wakefulness at all. It was now just a matter of time. Not knowing how much was the difficult part.

Still, his mother spent every day at her husband's bedside, holding his hand and reading to him from whatever book she had at her disposal. The days turned into weeks. Junior had made frequent visits over the summer and into the fall, always making sure not to cross paths with his brother. It was for the best. Juniour also decided not to head south for work that year.

With the first snowfall came the news from the doctor that his father had developed pneumonia and his body was beginning to shut down. He wasn't expected to last the week. So began the twenty-four hour vigil, taking shifts to make sure he would not die alone. The last day, Junior had stayed through the night, holding his father's hand, listening to his breathing become increasingly more laboured and jagged.

As the body weakens and the heart is no longer strong enough to push blood sufficiently, intelligent design kicks in and the blood vessels begin to rewire themselves, cutting off the supply from the hands and feet to conserve energy and restricting blood flow to the crucial organs housed in the body's core. The mottling would creep its way up his father's legs as the vessels shut down. When Junior arrived just before midnight the discolouration had begun on the toes and tops of the feet. By morning, it had extended above the ankles and was working its way up the calves.

He and his mother arrived just after nine.

"I'm gonna go crash on your couch for a few hours," Junior said as he hugged his mother. "Call me if there's any change or if you need anything."

They spent the morning sitting and watching as his father's abdomen struggled to rise and fall. There were moments when the time between one exhale and the next inhale was excruciatingly long before another rumbled intake of air shook his father's frail body.

He found himself drifting back in his memory, trying to grasp those nostalgic moments he had shared with his father. The attempt to do so was disconcerting. All of the glimpses into the past were of the time before Junior was born. There had been no special moments since, other than a dinner in a Ramada Inn. This realization only upset him.

He looked at his watch. "Mom, it's after twelve. Maybe we should go get something to eat."

They decided to go to a coffee shop across the street.

No.

They didn't go. His mother said she wasn't really hungry just yet and they should wait another hour. Fortunately, they remained at the bedside.

Just before one o'clock, his mother was sitting on the edge of the bed with her husband's hand clasped gently between her own. His father opened his eyes and looked at her. There was recognition. He knew who she was. He moved his lips and his mother leaned in to hear.

"Love you," he said, just above a whisper; then his eyes closed as he took a breath. He took another. That was all. He slipped away.

Less than a year later, his mother died – of a broken heart.

51

A taser delivers high voltage and low amperage to the human body. Police-grade weapons can discharge up to fifty thousand volts in an open arc, though only twelve hundred volts are actually delivered when the weapon has been activated. Electrodes, with small barbed darts attached, launch through the air at the victim. The victim's body completes the circuit. The resulting neuromuscular incapacitation, an over-stimulation of neurons, causes both pain and a cessation of motor control. The victim collapses.

You make it thirty feet down the hallway before you are hit. There was a second guard. You feel the sting as the barbs penetrate your abdomen, just before the charge rips your insides apart. Every muscle in your body is yanked toward your core. You swear you are having a heart attack. You drop to the floor. The current stops. You look up into the void. You are laughing. "I could see you," you say through a painful smile with saliva dribbling from the side of your mouth. "I – COULD – SEE – YOU!"

As the electricity was flowing from the weapon into your body, the arc of the current was visible. It is the first light you have seen in months. You are not blind. There have been many moments of doubt, but now you know for certain you still have your sight. You are ecstatic, delirious.

The approaching guard triggers a second burst that makes your brain sizzle. But again, you can see. This time you see something that helps you understand. You see that your captor's eyes are covered by some sort of apparatus, and then you recognize the night vision lenses. They can see you. They have always been able to see you.

"I can see you, too," you smile.

The guard you assaulted at the door joins the other. They drag you back into the cell. One of them disappears for a few minutes. After his return, they bind your hands above your head, and hoisting you to the low ceiling, lash the bonds to the rebar. They tie your feet to a three-foot separator pole, with one ankle strapped at either end. Your legs cannot support you. All of your weight hangs from your wrists. You give in to it.

Before they rip the electrodes from your stomach, they give you one more short burst for good measure, then they leave and slam the door behind them.

You are alone, again, thrown back into the pitch.

You whisper, "I can see."

52

My mother died of a broken heart. Was that too much? Too overly romanticized? Too clichéd? She did, though, both figuratively and literally.

After Dad passed, she started to withdraw from the world. She had already relinquished all of her volunteer work to spend her days with him in his last year, and saw no real point in returning to it after he'd gone. I guess she had lost her sense of purpose. Without a reason to live, she had given up. She withdrew into the confines of her condo, not going out very often. She wasn't eating properly, either. I'm not really sure how she spent her time.

Much of her life had been devoted to the care of others. For a short while, it had been taking care of me, though I didn't really need much. Junior was a gift to her selfless soul. He was a double-edged sword, I guess, with all of the challenges he presented, yet, he gave her a reason to get up each day and fight the good fight. But he grew up. Then came Dad's decline.

I tried my best to check in on her every few days. I tried to make sure I at least called her on the phone, but life is a boulder rolling down a hill. There were times when I just couldn't keep up.

The last time I saw her, I had taken her out for lunch on an October Tuesday. As we walked from her place to a diner in a mini-mall close by, she commented on the lovely colours of the changing leaves. She ordered a bowl of soup and nothing more. There wasn't much conversation as we ate. Her shoulders were tired and hunched and she seemed lost in her own thoughts.

I called her the next afternoon from work but there was no answer. I just figured she had gone out to buy groceries or to go for a walk. Thursday was a chaotic day at work, and I taught that evening. When I returned home there was some crisis requiring resolution with one of the girls. I had meant to phone, but life got in the way.

On Friday I received a call at work from the building manager at Mom's condo. One of her neighbours had complained of a vile smell coming through the vents from next door. The concern was that the sewer system had backed up. He had knocked but there was no response and wanted my permission to enter the premises. I told him I'd be right over.

He unlocked the door, but the security bar had been thrown. We had to force it, ripping it from the frame. I called for her in a panic as I crossed through the living room to the kitchen, then to her bedroom. Still no reply. The bathroom door was closed and locked. She lived alone and still locked the bathroom door. I had to kick it in.

There are things you don't talk about with other people, things that remain private. There are things you don't even discuss with yourself. You deliberately try to push them out of your head the best you can because they should not be dwelled upon.

Mom was lying on the tiled floor beside the tub in a pool of dried blood. She had been there for a while. Heart attack.

The coroner concluded either she had slipped and hit her head on the tub, causing the heart attack, or the heart attack had caused her to fall and hit her head on the tub. She had been there, on the bathroom floor, for three days.

    I should have called sooner. I should have gone over to check on her every day. I know nothing would have changed. She would still have died, but at least she wouldn't have been there... lying there... for three days. She died of a broken heart.

    There are things no one needs to know.

53

The police officer holding a radar gun waved him to the curb during the return trip. Because his eldest daughter had been running late, he had driven her to her part-time job. After dropping her off he turned right out of the parking lot into the right hand lane of a major four-lane street. Seeing the flashing lights of a police car stopped in the right lane several blocks ahead, he assumed someone had been pulled over. He looked for an opening in the traffic to slip into, to give the officer a safe amount of space. It's what a good citizen is supposed to do, isn't it? He was neck in neck with the vehicle beside him, and because no one was in front of either car, he accelerated to pull ahead and in front. Once there, he decelerated back down to the speed limit with two blocks to go.

Suddenly another officer from another police car hidden on a side street stepped out into the road and waved him over. He turned onto the side street and came to a stop. As the officer approached, he turned off the radio and rolled down his window.

"Sir," the young officer began with a condescending grin, "do you realize you were doing seventy-one in a fifty?"

He looked back over his shoulder to the main street. The police cruiser with flashers on was still sitting in the right lane but there was no other vehicle in front of it, nor, he now realized, had there ever been. The car was an obstacle to force drivers to accelerate to change lanes. It was a well-conceived speed trap.

"Your licence and registration, please."

He complied, and as he handed the documents through the window he said, "End of the month, I see."

"I'm sorry, sir?" came the confrontational response.

"Haven't hit the monthly quota for speeding tickets for the month so you set a trap. I get it."

The officer tensed up then turned and strode briskly to his vehicle to write up the violation. When the officer handed him back his papers and the ticket for a hundred and one dollars, he said, "You have thirty days to either pay the fine or contest it in court. You have the right to contest it, sir, but I'm just doing my job."

"I will be exercising my right, sir," and he rolled up the window, started the ignition, and continued home.

"Traffic court is such a waste of time and taxpayer money," he thought as he sat in a very uncomfortable chair. "The ticketing officer has to be present, so he's on the clock, sitting in here for over an hour, waiting for the case to be called when he should be out protecting and serving." He knew most people would just suck it up and pay the fine, but it just wasn't in his nature.

When the case number was called, they both walked forward and stood before the judge. "Talk about working your way up from the bottom," he thought. "Who would want to actually be assigned as a judge in traffic court? Or was it a punishment, a demotion?" The officer presented the details of the offence, with some major omissions. Then it was his turn.

"On what grounds do you contest the speeding ticket?" The unenthusiastic judge probably repeated this question hundreds of times, day after day.

He was more than prepared. He had even practiced in front of a mirror. He presented his version of events to the judge, pointing out the blatant entrapment involved, citing the interference of the police cruiser in the right lane, and describing the volume of traffic. "Of course someone would be forced to accelerate beyond the speed limit to avoid a collision with the police cruiser. I would also like to point out the date of the infraction being the twenty-ninth of the month."

"I'm not sure I see the relevance in the date," the judge challenged, leaning forward on the desk.

"It is obvious the police department was falling short on its quota of speeding tickets for the month, and this officer's assignment for the day was to make quota."

"I'm sorry, sir, but that is speculation on your part and has no bearing..."

"Actually, your honour, it is not speculation." He reached into a folder and pulled out an article from the local paper written three months ago with the headline "Cash-strapped City Hall".

"I worked as a journalist for many years and one of my former colleagues wrote this. It outlines some of the ways local government intended to deal with its financial short-fall." He placed the article on the judge's desk, indicating a hi-lighted section: "...and we are encouraging local law enforcement to be more vigilant in their pursuit of fineable offences..."

"A quote from the mayor," he went on. "Sounds like the implementation of quotas to me."

He turned to the police officer. "Was your assignment for the day to set up a speed enforcement trap in order to make monthly quota?"

The officer began to stammer to the judge.

"And what if I told you an acquaintance of mine who works on the force was able to provide me with a copy of the daily roster from the morning of the transgression," he continued while tapping his finger of the closed folder, "where it details your assignment for that day with the words 'make quota' in hand writing beside your name?"

The judge broke in. "It seems there is sufficient reason to set the infraction aside. Thank you both for your time. Next case."

He walked to his car, very satisfied in his achievement, especially considering he had no copy of the roster in the folder he carried under his arm. His bluff could have gone very wrong, but he had learned if you speak with conviction, people tend to believe you even if you are full of shit.

54

Wait. That didn't happen, did it? Well, some of it did, but not the last part. The last part is what I told people at work. It was a better story, a better ending. No one wants to hear, "...so I paid the fine." An inconsequential anecdote with an improved ending takes on new dimensions, expresses rebellion and hope. Besides, people are forgiving of intentional fabrications when they involve pulling a fast one on the powers that be, those who usually take advantage of the little guy.

Yet, I've told this story so many times, there are moments when I actually believe it's the truth. But it's just a story. I admit it, but no one wants to hear a boring story. A boring story means a boring life. We all do it. I listen to people who do it every day, creative embellishment.

We're all just the sum of our stories. On the vertical is the truth, or at least our version of the truth. On the horizontal are the fictions we create to hold the truths together. The strands are woven to form the sackcloth of who we are. When the weave is pulled tight, sometimes it's hard to differentiate between the horizontal and the vertical.

We remove the hurting parts, those which cause us

pain, those which remind us of our failures, or those which display our inability to overcome. We re-write those stories to make ourselves feel better and to boost our often lacking confidence so we can survive the mundanity of life.

Because I have nothing but time for reflection, I am picking at some of those loose strands in the fabric and seeing them for what they really are, and my life for what it really is as the fabric unravels. Maybe reality is the real hell.

55

Everyone needs a purpose. Goals are different. Goals are the benchmarks, the progressive steps on the path to a purpose. The French use the term *raison d'être* – the reason to be, to exist.

His purpose was to share stories. He always wrote, and his benchmarks took him down the path through rungs of journalism. He was forced to veer into the publishing industry, but that occupation still fed his passions. There were still goals on the horizon, one of which was to become an author. It was the retirement plan, and in whatever spare time he had, he wrote. Every career choice he made was to that hopeful end.

Life involves relationships, and relationships can become challenges that interfere with individual purpose, especially when the other person in the relationship has a purpose that is quite different.

Sometimes, people realize what they thought they wanted is not as fulfilling as they expected it to be. What happens if, in the relationships that develop, they are not up front about their true intentions? What if they lead others down the wrong path?

He thought his wife wanted to be a stylist. She had spoken, in those first few months of their relationship, of owning her own salon one day in a big city. Maybe she believed it at the time, or maybe she just saw the job as one of the goals toward her real purpose.

In hindsight, he should have known all she really wanted was for someone to save her from a life in a hick railroad town. She did not have the confidence in herself to make the move on her own. Her plan was to become a mother of children with a husband who could provide in a better place. She might have loved him. She probably thought she did; or perhaps she just loved the idea of him. With his plans and aspirations he was her opportunity to escape. He was a golden ticket; maybe not golden, but at least, a means to an end. There was nothing malicious or premeditated in her plan. It was what it was.

He had seen their relationship as an opportunity to share his life with someone instead of ending up alone and lonely. That was his greatest fear. It was all quite symbiotic in the beginning.

Things change. The pending arrival of their first baby was all so new and exciting. After the wedding they moved from the tiny one-bedroom apartment into a townhouse rental. They decorated the nursery on weekends and evenings and bought all the requisite sleepers, diapers, and other accoutrements to prepare for their leap into parenthood. They read books on parenting and went to birthing classes.

The first few weeks after the birth were joyous, buoyed by the adrenaline of change. But adrenaline has a tendency to run out. He was back at work and she was becoming increasingly sleep-deprived. She insisted on breast-feeding. He did not disagree, and tried to help out with middle-of-the-night feedings.

The repetitive nature of caring for a newborn was wearing her down, as was the isolation of being at home all day with the baby. She did not have a circle of friends with small children for companionship and support. He hadn't previously noticed that, in fact, she didn't really have any friends at all. Her mother came by when she could to help out, but she worked full-time and had issues of her own to deal with on the relationship front.

There were days when he could work from home, writing articles, but much of his job required him to be out in the community, gathering information and conducting interviews that would become the columns on the page.

He came home unannounced one afternoon to find his wife curled up on the bathroom floor crying, while the baby was in her playpen at full wail.

He tried to console her but she would have none of it. She snapped at him. "I can have a bad day, can't I?" Then she sent him back to work with, "I don't need your help."

Her downward spiral of exhaustion and moodiness did not improve even after the baby was sleeping through the night. He tried to get her to talk about whatever was bothering her but whenever he started to broach the subject, she would shut him down with, "I'm fine." She was always fine.

He didn't know what to do for her. All he ever wanted was for her to be happy.

He had been applying for work with newspapers in larger markets and just a few months before Sport turned two, an offer came in from a newspaper in a large community five hours away. Because the paper was a subsidiary of a larger media organization, the opportunity was exciting. If his writing were good enough and the stories he was covering were engaging enough, the result might be syndication. The chances of shifting to a large city paper within the company's fold, or even into television, loomed on the horizon of possibilities.

He accepted the offer, packed up their small family, and headed south. During the move, his wife informed him she was pregnant again. This time of change brought her a new sense of optimism. She was finally leaving her hometown for greener pastures.

Her happiness was short-lived. They now lived in a large town. His new job was much more demanding of his time and energy, and when Einstein was born, his wife was left at home with two children under the age of three to care for.

She thought the move would make life better. She thought the challenges would all become easier to overcome. She thought motherhood was her *raison d'être*. Instead of experiencing the satisfaction she had hoped for, all she felt was the drudgery, and the isolation in an unfamiliar environment, with no connection to the community, and no real aspirations for her own future. This escape from small town life was supposed to be all she had ever wanted.

While her life stalled, his flourished. His increasing responsibilities at work consumed more of his time. Assignments required his attendance at town hall meetings during the evenings. Stories breaking on the weekends necessitated his on-site presence. He justified his absence from home by thinking he was establishing himself in his vocation, providing for his family in material and financial ways.

When he was secure enough in his position, they bought a house in the suburbs in a neighbourhood close to the church his wife had become involved with the previous year. He was grateful she had found something to belong to, a community she could connect with. As the mother of little girls aged five and two, she was becoming a frustrated yeller and a spanker. Church gave her some sense of peace that she was lacking.

The new house had a side entrance into a finished

basement. Thinking that a part-time return to hairdressing might be good for her, he suggested that she open up her own hair salon down there.

"And what am I supposed to do with the children while I cut hair?" He suggested they put the girls in daycare for one day a week to start, or hire a nanny. Although she rejected his proposal at first, she finally conceded that a job might be the answer. At least it would be something different.

He hired a contractor to do the renovation. Their life seemed to settle down for a couple of years. It was not a life of togetherness, but it was at least functional. Neither of them realized how disconnected they had become. The status quo became comfortable, and just when the ship appeared to be on an even keel, it was time for the winds to change once again.

She wanted another baby. With Sport now in school full time and Einstein starting grade one the following year, she realized how empty the house and her life would be. He was skeptical. He knew what a difficult time she had experienced with their first two daughters and his own work schedule was now unrelenting. Yet, he thought she did seem more settled of late. He was afraid of her becoming listless, and plunging once again into dark seas without a rudder. So he agreed.

At the end of her first trimester, the cosmos threw them yet another curve. He was offered a position with a national publication. His acceptance would require the family to move to the city, and him to travel more. This was the opportunity he had been waiting for. His hard work had paid off and he was receiving recognition for those efforts.

"You'll have to turn it down," she stated when he presented the news to her at dinner.

"But this is what I've always wanted. This is what I was meant to do."

"We are not uprooting the children just so you can take a job where you will *never* be at home. No. This is not an option. You can take it if you want to, but the girls and I are staying put."

There had never been such a definite line drawn in the sand in their relationship. While his plans in the past were serving her purposes, she was fine going along for the ride. Her ultimatum implied the end of their marriage if he moved forward with the offer. He was at a loss. He thought he had done everything right, worked hard to improve their life, made good choices, supported her to the best of his ability. Now he was faced with two options: a failed marriage or an abandoned dream.

He was the responsible one.

His employers at the daily publication were quite disappointed in his decision. This opportunity had been offered to him because of the writing on the wall regarding the future of the newspaper. A major downsize was inevitable because of falling sales and subscriptions. He had recognized the decline too, but he thought his experience and seniority would keep him safe. The opposite was true. When the time came to cut the fat, he was one of the highest paid reporters, and the first one to be let go. He was given a decent severance and a handshake just as the ownership of the paper changed hands; even his own bosses hadn't seen that one coming.

He was in his early thirties and suddenly his career was over. If he were going to try to keep working in the news business, the family would definitely have to move.

"I'm sure you can find work doing something related right here in town," was the only comfort she had to offer. She didn't have any awareness of how ridiculous a statement it was. He began to resent her.

Only through good fortune and the contacts he had

made through the newspaper did he find work with Smyth Publishing. He was a writer, not an editor, but this career change would be necessary.

Two weeks after Princess was born, he left work at his new job a bit early. He had an appointment at a clinic to get a vasectomy. It was a decision he made on his own, one he chose not to share with his wife.

56

Three days. They have left you hanging from the ceiling for three days. No food. No water.

The least they could have done was to remove your pants so you didn't have to shit and piss in them. You tried not to for the first day, but the taser had done quite a number on your intestines. Your bladder let go with the first burst. Maybe it's a good thing you haven't eaten, nothing for your body to void.

Your mouth is so dry, though. Your lips are cracked and you taste blood from them. Everything aches. You've lost most of the feeling in your arms. Your fingers are freezing from lack of circulation. The leather straps on your wrists aren't too tight; it's the weight of your body causing them to dig into your wrists. You can take the weight off by standing awkwardly, but then your back goes into spasms because you have to hunch over for so long. When you sleep, your wrists take all of your weight.

You had to try to get out. You had to. Did they expect you to linger here forever and not try? This is your torture. These are the devils. Dehydration. Starvation. Bondage.

Wrapped in your own excrement and urine.

When will this end? They have to let you down sometime, don't they? Have things changed? Does it matter to them now if you die or not? You start thinking about the possibility that this is how your life will end, a slow death of lingering starvation. How horrible will that be? You can only imagine. And you do. It terrifies you.

It was a good thing you tried to do. Your escape attempt showed courage, and you know best of all that no good deed goes unpunished. You start begging them to let you down, apologizing for your transgression. "I'm sorry I tried to get out. It won't happen again. I promise."

Stop being so pathetic. You stood up to them. It's all you ever wanted to do in your life, to stand up to people. What are you apologizing for? This is who you have always claimed you have been.

Or is it?

57

I wish I could say I missed sex. I do miss it, but not because I've been thrown in here. It had already become nonexistent in my marriage. I have had thoughts, fantasies, causing arousal. The mind wanders where it wanders, but I've pushed those thoughts away. They serve no purpose here.

The beginning of our relationship was passionate, as new relationships often are. Having a child tends to put a damper on intimacy, so that change was expected. Things improved again when the desire for a second child kicked in. I was only mildly aware of that decision. We hadn't discussed it in actual words, but when the frequency of our sexual intimacy increased, I suspected the decision had been made for me. I wasn't opposed to having another baby, so I didn't question her plan, even though she was not in a positive emotional space. I just thought a new baby would make things better for her because it was something she wanted.

After our second child was born, precautions were reinstated and opportunities dwindled. After children become independently mobile, they wander into their parents' bedroom if they waken during the night. Nobody wants to be in the middle of a moment if that occurs, so the moments were minimized.

Also, my work a got in the way: making love after I returned home at midnight to my sleeping wife was not a welcomed option. She became angry if I woke her up to instigate even a hug. Sleep was a more valued commodity than physical contact. Of course, frequency returned with the decision to have a third, but it was all very pragmatic and functional. Its purpose was purely procreative. Then it ceased.

There was a brief flirtation with the thought of having a fourth child. "Wouldn't you like to try to have a son?" she asked one evening when Princess was two.

"I don't think we need any more." Finances were tight with the new job. We had to sell the second vehicle. I was making less than when I worked at the newspaper and I had just taken on a teaching position at the college to be able to provide for the extras.

I guess she decided if we weren't going to have any more children, there was no longer a reason to have sex. A silent oath of celibacy had been sworn and I didn't get the memo.

When Princess went through a bout of night terrors, my wife began sleeping with her in her single bed just in case she woke up in distress. I asked if she was ever going to return to our bedroom.

"It just a phase she's going through," she replied. "But I have been sleeping much better with her. Since you've put on the extra pounds, your snoring is worse. Maybe you should take better care of yourself."

A few months later I came home from work to find that my wife had moved our queen bed into Princess's room and had set up Princess' twin bed in our room. I guess it was just my room now.

58

He was running errands on a Saturday afternoon, just the usual stuff. He had been given a list. He planned out a route.

His wife and daughters had gone to visit her mother for the weekend so he thought he'd grab some dinner and take in a movie after he was done.

He had just finished shopping at the mall, and was driving through the parking lot toward the exit. As he passed by the grocery store at the west end he saw her standing there, Irish, with a cartload of groceries waiting for something, probably a ride. He pulled up beside her and rolled down the passenger side window.

"Hello there," he said, smiling. "Just waiting for your husband to bring the car around?"

"Oh, hi," she smiled back. "No. Waiting for a cab. My husband's off on business and he has the car."

"Well, can I offer you a ride? I think it's on my way."

"Oh, that would be lovely. You're sure it isn't any bother?"

"I've got nothing to do today and nowhere else to be."

He got out and helped her load her bags into the trunk.

"Just let me know where I'm going." He couldn't seem to wipe the smile from his face.

"Well, *you* seem to be in a very good mood today," she commented, noticing his expression.

"It's just a great day off is all. My family's out of town and I seem to have the day all to myself. It's kinda nice for a change."

They made small talk about work for the duration of the drive with her breaking in now and then to inform him of when he needed to make the next left or right. She lived in a fifteen-storey condominium complex close to downtown. He pulled up at the front entrance.

"Actually," she said, "would you be able to give me a hand getting all these bags up to my flat. It usually takes me two trips."

"Sure thing."

"You can park over there, in the visitor section."

After he had pulled in to an available spot, they unloaded the bags, each of them taking three on each arm. He awkwardly closed the trunk with his chin and followed her through the main lobby into the elevators. Her condo was on the twelfth floor. It was a contemporary bright space with large windows from floor to ceiling in the living room. There was a dining area off to the right with an open kitchen just beyond a breakfast bar. He assumed the bedroom and bathroom were off to the left. They unburdened themselves, placing the bags on the bar.

"Thank you so much for your help. I really do appreciate it."

"Oh, my pleasure. Well, if that's everything, I guess I'll be on my way." He started towards the door.

"Can I offer you something to drink? Coffee, tea? I have some wine if you'd prefer."

He wasn't going to refuse an opportunity to linger. "Well, OK. Wine would be good."

She poured them each a glass of red and they sat together on the couch.

They had never engaged in conversation before other than job-related details at work. He asked about her family and when they had moved from Ireland. She gave him the Reader's Digest version: the highlights of her life that brought her to the present. He did the same. She poured more wine and the conversation flowed freely.

It was almost surreal. She was a beautifully voluptuous woman and he could listen to her voice and her laugh for hours. In fact, he did.

After the third glass of wine, he realized the sun was getting low in the sky.

"Look at the time," he said to her. "Perhaps I should be on my way."

She rose from the couch. "Just hold on for a moment. I'll be right back," she said as she headed off toward the bedroom.

When she returned, she was naked. She stood in the doorway with a coy look upon her face. "Do you like what you see?" she asked.

He did.

It was an unforgettably fantastic evening.

59

Everyone has regrets. People who tell you they don't are definitely lying. Life is too rife with decision-making to avoid doubts about choices made. Most regrets are about things done or said in the heat of the moment, without thought of consequence.

My regrets mostly revolve around the things I *didn't* do, the opportunities I *didn't* seize because there was too much risk involved, too much to lose for a short-term benefit. I regret not taking chances, not walking on the road less travelled.

I did not cheat on my wife that evening even though I wanted to. I so wanted to. In my mind, I did, many times. When Irish came out of the bedroom, she was wearing a lovely silk nightgown with thin straps over her bare shoulders. She was absolutely stunning.

"I know it's wrong of me to ask – I know we're both married – but would you like to…"

I stood there facing one of the greatest decisions of my life. It is incredible how, within the course of a few seconds, I ran through a myriad of possible scenarios in my head. I knew I would get caught. I didn't know if my wife would even care anymore, but on principle she would leave me and take the girls with her. She would see my infidelity as a golden opportunity. There would be a divorce and I would lose everything, all for an evening of fleeting pleasure.

Yet, the idea of an evening of pleasure certainly had its appeal considering I had not been with my wife in almost three years. Here stood a woman who wanted to be with me, physically, though I could not even come close to imagining why. I was no one's catch. Perhaps she saw me as someone safe, someone who had too much to lose in anything more than a frivolous fling, someone who looked desperate enough to not turn down her invitation. I can't imagine anyone doing that – other than me.

"I am truly flattered and I find you incredibly attractive," I told her, "but I am married and I have three beautiful daughters. I love my wife and…"

But I didn't love my wife. In that moment, as those words came out of my mouth, I knew they were a lie. My wife and I hadn't loved each other in years, but we were all each other had.

"I understand," she said. "I'm sorry. I just thought maybe…"

As I got into my car and drove away, I realized I had just created the greatest regret of my life; another safe, uninteresting choice among a long list of safe, uninteresting choices.

60

On the fourth day they let you down. You hear the key in the lock and feel the breeze of fresh, stale air as the door swings out. Without words they come in and cut you down from the rebar. You have no strength to fight or even stand; you simply drop. They don't even try to support you. They remove your leg restraints and the straps around your wrists. They strip you of your soiled clothes.

Before they go, you hear the familiar sound of a paper plate being placed on the floor and a bottle of water being set down beside it. So, you have either been forgiven or punished enough for your transgression.

Your arms burn as they lie at your side. The muscles are unfamiliar with this new position. You try to roll over onto your stomach so you can crawl over to the food and water, but your arms will not cooperate. They are bags of burning jelly. You will have to give your body time to adjust. You are not hungry at all. Your stomach is still too messed up to even think about food, but water is needed.

Thinking about death for four days has sapped you of any desire to live. You see death as the ultimate escape, a release from your suffering, just as it was with your father in the end.

You stink. Everything stinks. You even smell like death, like the acrid odour that hit you when you broke through your mother's bathroom door. Your stench makes you gag, then dry heave. There is nothing in your stomach to bring up.

Why is this all happening to you? None of it makes any sense. It never has. You are nothing, nobody. You just want to go back to sleep. When you sleep, you are gone from this place. When you sleep, you don't feel anything, you don't think about anything. Thinking has become dangerous. You don't like what you've been learning about who you are, who you thought you were.

In this space, you are ceasing to exist, but did you ever really exist in the first place?

61

Let me tell you a lie.

One night in university I had been out drinking with some of the guys from my floor in residence. We were all feeling no pain as we stumbled our way home after closing out one of the local drinking holes.

University bars are not the most high-end establishments and are also not located in the best parts of town. This neighbourhood was pretty sketchy.

We were staggering down one particularly dark street that had seen better days. Small, two-storey wartime houses sat behind overgrown front yards, littered with rusty bicycles and broken toys. Most of them were low-income rentals managed by some slumlord who did the bare minimum to maintain them.

Up ahead we heard someone yelling, a man. We couldn't make out the words at first, but the tone was snide and angry. As we approached we heard a woman's voice, too. It was filled with fear. The couple was on the decrepit front porch of one of the houses. He was screaming profanities at her, calling her a stupid bitch and asking her if she thought she could keep it from him. He must have hit her at least once because she was cowering at the far end of the porch, leaning on the rail, protecting her head with her hands.

"I'll show you," the man growled as he went inside the house. He returned quickly with a small jerrycan in his hands. He opened one end and proceeded to douse the woman in gasoline.

Seeing this, my pals and I decided to intervene, the booze having made us brave. I took the lead and, stepping through the rotting wooden gate, made a beeline for the man. The others followed.

"Whoa down there, buddy," I slurred slightly as I reached the steps.

"Butt out. This is none o' your fuckin' business. Get off my property."

"I really think you should leave her alone."

"Oh, you do, do ya? Well, do something about it."

I grabbed him by the collar of his black leather jacket and dragged him off the porch. Everything had happened so fast that my drunken university pals could not process and just stood there at the gate, watching in awe. I managed to avoid getting punched by swinging the guy off balance. I used my extra weight to my advantage. I got a leg in behind him and tripped him up, causing us both to topple to the patchwork lawn.

I struggled to get on top, and just as I was about to punch the guy in the face, I was hit across the back with something hard, a broom handle that cracked upon impact. I turned to see the woman I had stepped in to defend getting ready to take another swing at me with a now jagged piece of broom handle. She screamed at me, "You leave him the fuck alone, you fucking asshole. This is none of your goddamned business. Get the fuck out of here," then she swung again.

I rolled off him just in time and scrambled back to the gate, yelling at her, "You are fuckin' nuts. I was trying to help. You deserve what you get, you stupid cow."

I have told that story dozens of times and it changes a little bit with each telling, depending on which parts of the story people react to the most positively, but it's not true. Well, it's not my story. Oh, it happened, just not to me. It is plagiarism at its finest.

It should have been my story. They had asked me to go out drinking with them that night, but I said no. I was always being the conscientious student, rarely going out in lieu of studying or writing the next paper. I always played it safe, never took any risks, never had any fun. I always did what was expected of me, never causing anyone any conflict or concern. I have no stories to tell of interesting things I've done or adventures I've been on, because they don't exist. When you tow the line, there's nothing to tell.

But who wants to admit to an uneventful life? Who wants to say he has done nothing of any significance? I haven't lived. I've just passed through by keeping my head down and my nose clean. I wanted my life to be interesting, but I never learned how.

62

Is this the point where I should consider prayer? Should I ask God for forgiveness for my sins and beg for his or her assistance in my emancipation? Or do I try to make a deal? Promise the Lord I will change my ways in exchange for my freedom? No one ever really changes. Besides, that would truly make me a hypocrite.

My parents never took us to church. It had never been part of my world until my wife found Jesus. Actually, I don't even know if she found Jesus. I think she just found a place to be. I guess it's all anyone is looking for.

I remember thinking about the existence of God when I was a kid. I didn't have all the vocabulary I needed to explain how I felt at the time, but in high school I stumbled upon the words that nailed it in an historical anthology of Greek philosophers.

I was drawn to the Epicurean Paradox, which states: "Is God willing to prevent evil, but not able? Then he is not omnipotent. Is he able, but not willing? Then he is malevolent. Is he both able and willing? Then whence cometh evil? Is he neither able nor willing? Then why call him God?" Epicurus knew exactly how I felt, and nothing I have seen in this world has changed my mind, especially my current situation.

There seems to be no end in sight. I know that events in life have a beginning, a middle, and an end; even when I am going through some kind of trial or tribulation, therefore, I can usually see a light at the end of the tunnel.

So much of my life has worked that way. School always had a beginning, middle, and an end. Every assignment worked that way. Every news story I covered and wrote. Every book I've edited. Every story I've told or read.

The one real thing I was able to contribute that helped my wife through three labours: I reminded her, with every contraction, that it wouldn't last long. I kept reminding her that the pain would eventually end, and when it was all over, we would have a beautiful baby as our reward.

There is no light in this tunnel. There is no light at all. There was no real beginning either, not one I can remember. I am, quite simply, stuck in the middle.

Is any of this even real? What if there is no end? What if it is not finite? Is this for eternity? Maybe I'm already dead and Danté was right.

63

The brothers agreed to spend the weekend clearing out their mother's condo. She had been true to her word: every item she owned had a piece of masking tape stuck to it designating who the recipient should be. She had been meticulous, and even revealed her often hidden sense of humour. The pepper shaker had his name on the bottom, but the salt shaker was labeled "Junior." Items she knew neither of them would want were marked "Junk." She was right on the money with all of those. At some point she had even divided all of the photographs into separate boxes for each of them. They didn't talk much. The elephant was still very present. They focused on the task, often becoming distracted by some of the lost treasures which led them down nostalgic side paths of memory.

Junior had borrowed a friend's van to load up the "junk" to drop off at one of the local charities. For the last time, Junior slept on his mother's couch. On Sunday night the place was empty. They stood in the centre of the hollow living room.

"Well, I guess this is it," Junior broke the uncomfortable silence.

"I guess so." He paused. "It's going on the market tomorrow. The realtor suggested a price just below market so it will sell quickly."

"Right. Good idea."

"I'm meeting with the lawyer next week to get all the details of the will settled. Once this place sells it should be a simple process."

"Good. Let me know if you need anything from me."

"I won't. I mean everything's pretty cut and dried."

They stood across the room from each other. There were words hanging in the air between them but neither wanted to be the one to reach out and grab them.

"You heading back tonight?"

"Yep. Nothing keepin' me here."

"Well... Have a safe drive."

"I will."

This was their relationship: two brothers at opposite ends of a room filled with empty space.

He drove to the city after all the legal details had been settled. He thought about just mailing his brother the cheque, his half of the estate. However, that seemed at bit cold, so he gave Junior a call to make sure he would be at home. He also needed Junior's address. They had never been to each other's houses.

"Come on in," Junior said as he cleared the doorway for his brother to pass.

"I'm not here for long." He didn't make a move to enter. "I just wanted to make sure you got this in person," handing his brother an unmarked envelope.

Junior stepped out on to the porch. "Thank you." He looked at the envelope, folded it in half, and tucked it into his back pocket.

"Aren't you going to open it?"

"If it will make you happy." He retrieved the envelope from one pocket, took a penknife from another, and slit it open. He removed the cheque and looked at the amount. His eyes lingered there for a moment. There was no change in his expression. He looked up. "Happy now?"

"Do you have any questions?"

"Nope."

"OK. Good. I guess that's it then."

"I guess so. Goodbye, brother."

64

When Mom started to withdraw from the world after Dad died, I began to notice things when I'd visit. She wasn't taking care of herself. Her fridge didn't have much food in it. Laundry was left in piles. I would notice layers of dust forming on shelves, and unopened bills on the kitchen table.

So, after some discussion, I arranged for someone to come in once a week to clean and do laundry for her. I took her out each week to get groceries. We went to the bank and added my name to all of her accounts so I could make sure all the bills were getting paid on time.

This arrangement gave us both peace of mind.

Far too often, people make decisions based on emotion and sentiment, leaving logic out of the equation. They think they are doing what will be fair for everyone concerned without considering the realities. As a result, problems and disappointments tend to develop.

When my parents wrote their wills, they were guided by their hearts and not their heads. I understood that, even if I didn't agree. They weren't being realistic. They didn't see that I was supporting a family of five almost all on my own. Junior had no dependents. Therefore, during the year before Mom passed, I leveled the playing field. I bled off money from her investments when they matured and moved it into education funds for my girls. I had to look out for their futures. It's what a father does. There would still be plenty left over for Junior.

When I took him his cheque, there was more to the conversation. As I turned to leave, he stopped me.

"Actually, I do have a question. How ignorant do you really think I am?"

"What?" I asked. "I don't know what you're talking about."

"Really? Do you think you are so high and mighty, so much more important than me you really believe Mum and Dad didn't share things with me, too?"

"I still have no idea what you are talking about."

"Wow. You are somethin' else." He leaned back on the door frame and crossed his arms over his chest. "Mum gave me the same package she gave you when Dad broke his hip. I know how much their estate should have been worth."

"Look. You don't know what you're talking about. Some of their investments took a big hit in the last couple of years. It happens."

But they both knew.

"That's your story and you're stickin' to it? Really?"

"It's not a story. It's the truth." I had figured he wouldn't question how much money he inherited; he'd simply be happy to receive anything, given the way he lived and the choices he'd made. "Look, if you need me to, I can provide you with all the paperwork showing the total worth of the estate. I can have the lawyer send you copies of all that…"

"Don't bother. It's not about the money. You just don't get it, do you? You never have and you never will." He thought for a moment. "Do you know why you were a good reporter?

'Cause you never formed any emotional attachment to any of your stories. I read a lot of them. Just the facts, black and white, never any room for grey."

I just stood there, staring at him.

"We all have to live with our choices. You're just fooling yourself, not me. I know what you are. You think you're always right all the time. You always have to be right, don't you? Well, good luck with that, brother."

Junior went back into his house and slammed the door.

It was the last time we spoke.

65

You have become quite pathetic, really. You are curled up on your side on the concrete floor with your blanket under your head. You haven't moved for hours. The food you haven't eaten still sits by the door and you've only been sipping at your water. You are lost in your own thoughts, oblivious to the nothingness around you.

What are you thinking about? All the things you miss? Are you *still* doing that? We talked about this. There's no point. You are never getting out of here. Haven't you figured it out yet? They have no intention of ever letting you go. You are at the bottom. You have no hope left. Now you have an inkling of where Jarrod Turning found himself. You remember him, don't you? He is the young man who dropped your class, devastated by the end of a relationship. At least he knew how to love deeply.

You sit up and hold your head in your hands. You want to stop thinking, but you can't, can you? Your hands move to cover your ears in the hopes of blocking out my voice, but it's not working, is it? You will never be able to shut me out.

Out of the Pitch

I am you. You are me. We are him.

I know you want to end it all. You are trying to think of ways to do that, but your options are limited. You could stop drinking and eating, I suppose, but dying would be a slow, lengthy process. You think about ripping your potato sack clothes into strips and tying a noose to the rebar, but that method won't work, either, will it? They're probably watching you as well as listening. There's probably an infrared camera just above the rebar in the ventilation shaft. You think about trying to escape again in the hopes that in the process of stopping you, they will kill you.

Here's an idea: let the scorpions get you. Oh, that wouldn't work either. You've never really been anaphylactic. Just another embellishment for the sake of a better story, to build empathy for the protagonist, wasn't it?

You've figured out how to deal with the scorpions. You can see them with your ears. It's become a sick game to you now. You can hear where they are and which direction they're moving. You've learned to attack from the rear, slowly sneaking up behind them with your own pincers, nabbing their tails between your thumb and index finger. It's simple enough now. You drop them down the drain. If the fable holds true, they can't swim and they drown. It does hold true. You drop them in, you hear the plop as they hit the surface, and they don't return. That's really your only amusement, your only success. Excellent. You know how to kill a scorpion in the dark.

No one will ever know this great accomplishment except for *you, me, and him – we.*

Your life unravels like a sweater. If you look closely enough, you will find an imperfection in the knit. You'll try to ignore it, but it grabs your attention and you start to pick at it. Next thing you know, you've pulled it too hard and one row starts to come undone, then the next, and the next, until the sweater is nothing but a pile of yarn on the floor. That's what you look like now: a pile of yarn on the floor with only a few more rows of the sweater left intact.

Why don't *we* finish the job?

66

He never confronted that son-of-a-bitch of a teacher. The last time he saw him was at his high school graduation. It's so ironic: the man who shook his hand and gave him his diploma was the same one who told him he was never going to make it. Oh, he did go back to the school after graduation to confront him, but the son-of-a-bitch wasn't there that day. Apparently, he had played hooky to go fishing with his son. Even in his fabricated showdown he didn't win. The least you can do when you bullshit the end of a story is to have the protagonist overcome or outsmart the antagonist, but you couldn't even do that right.

His meeting with the dean... "If you're going to hold a gun to my head, make sure you pull the trigger." It's a line stolen from some movie. In his mind, he imposed it over top of the real conversation, the one where he feigned contrition and left the office with his tail firmly entrenched between his legs. Just another artist recycling old canvases, painting over the imperfections.

And his steamy sexual fantasy about Irish... No, not the first one; the second one. The fantasy where he does the right thing and turns her down... Yes, that was imagined, too; an extra layer of impressionist pigment. He drove right by her. He saw her standing there waiting for what he assumed was a cab and was just about to pull over, but lost his nerve at the last moment and drove away. You can't even have an erotic fantasy where you take risks. You always have to do the right thing, every fuckin' time.

Junior was so right about you.

What other webs have you woven?

Right. He isn't a fiction editor. Irish is. He works in non-fiction, proofreading for grammatical and spelling errors and being a fact-checker. They thought it was a good fit when they hired him based on all of his cold, emotionless articles: always well sourced and researched but lacking any real flavour or colour; all black or white, right or wrong.

Face it. He was the only one to apply to teach the creative writing course at the college. It's the only way he got the job: they were desperate. He can't even get his own novels published by the company he works for. The only reason Smyth said it would be a conflict of interest was because he was trying to let you down easy, something you've never considered doing with your own students.

What else? The list is just so long. Telling the girls the dog was "sent to the farm" when you accidentally ran him over? "Pulling the man from the wreckage and saving his life" when you witnessed that car crash at the intersection when out of town on business? How about some of those grades in university you "pulled off"?

Why are you rolling on the ground with your fingers in your ears? Don't you like what I'm saying? It's called the truth, after all, and we're not done yet, but I need to hear you say them: your words speaking the truth.

Confess! Not to any of the gods, just to yourself.

67

FINE!

My father never said he was proud of me. Ever. He must have been, though. I did everything right. I did what I was supposed to do. The night we went out for dinner when I was in university... we ate our meal in silence. We drank a few beers and made small talk about the weather, a little politics, and current events, but nothing of any substance. He paid the bill, said goodnight, and went back to his room. He wasn't even a bit tipsy. His visit offered the perfect opportunity for us to have a real conversation, just the two of us, and it didn't happen. I so wanted it to happen, for him to say the words. I knew he felt them, but I wanted to hear them.

And the one real thing about my father I have resented the most is the trait I have manifested in abundance: the aversion I have to face conflict and stand up for myself. I have become my father's son, indeed. I just lie and make up my own endings as I wish they could have been because I am so ashamed of my inability to accept them as they actually were.

In the end, he did die alone, my father. My mother and I didn't wait the extra hour before going to the coffee shop to grab some lunch. It was my fault. I shouldn't have suggested we go when I did, but I opened my stupid mouth and put the idea into the space and she said, "OK." When we returned to his room he had already gone. There was no "Love you," said to my mother. There was no holding of his hand when he passed. My words robbed her of that possible ending.

No one should die alone, especially my father… or my mother…

I'm going to die alone, too, aren't I?

Right here in the pitch.

It's where I belong.

68

I have been focused for so long on the idea – the hope - of being released back into my life, into freedom. The loss of freedom leads to the examination of personal losses.

What have I lost? I've lost working my ass off to make ends meet while others profit on the back of my efforts. I've lost feeling the need to keep up with the Joneses and the Smiths and the world telling me I'm not good enough the way I am, I don't wear the right clothes or drive the right car. I'm too heavy. I'm too bald. I've lost being responsible for everyone else around me, my family, my neighbours, my co-workers - everyone, always putting myself last. I've lost having to worry about the hell that is other people and their self-absorbed frivolities and inane, trite conversations. I've lost having to make mundane, meaningless decisions about superficial inconsequential matters. I've lost being a slave to societal expectation and consumerism. This is what I've lost.

You used to sit there missing elements of your life. Remember how you spent a whole day listing what you miss: The fresh crunch of an apple between your teeth, the first spring day when winter hibernation ends and you step outside of your house without jumping back in, the magnolia blossoms that soon follow, the aroma of freshly brewed Honduran coffee, the wind in your face as you ride your bike by the river, the smell of a bonfire in your backyard as you dispose of the fallen branches from numerous winter storms, the feeling of a fountain pen as it scratches the ink onto a page, waking from a wonderful dream on a Saturday morning when you had the opportunity sleep in.

You miss cherry ice cream, the spine cracking when you first open a new book, the snapping closed of a hardcover novel at the moment of completion, windy days, freshly pressed hotel bed sheets after a long flight, the first swig of Coke but not the rest of the can, losing yourself in a hot morning shower.

I told you to stop. Remember that? DO YOU REMEMBER? I told you nothing good would come from thinking about what you miss, because wanting makes it worse. Wanting sets you up for failure and frustration when the object of your desire remains forever out of reach, and it does, you know. It may give you a taste, a tiny nibble, just to keep you aching, but the goal, the dream, never becomes real and you remain unfulfilled and empty. "Want nothing," I told you, so you will never be disappointed ever again, especially here where you can have nothing. Want is not even an option.

So you stopped wanting and you saw that the real demons exist, just as Danté described, out of the pitch: the unpredictable continual torture in a world full of unrealistic expectations and failed aspirations.

And then it dawned on you, in that moment: you missed no one. There were no people on your list. You did not miss your wife or your children. There were no buddies you hung out with, no friend you met with for coffee. Sartre was right. Hell is other people.

    What is there to go back to?
    Yes, we're in hell, but it's a hell we know.
    This is freedom. The darkness embraces you, and I embrace the darkness.

69

You are lying on the cold cement floor breathing deeply in through the nose and out through the mouth. You are finally losing it. You have to ground yourself.

Your cell is a circle sixteen feet across. The metal door is four feet high. The hinges and handle are on the outside. The drainage hole in the centre of the floor is one foot wide. The ceiling is a dome five feet high with a similar grated hole above for ventilation. Food and water appear when you wake from sleep. You have a wool blanket and sackcloth clothes. This is your world, your reality. This is all there is.

You are a human, and humans adapt. You have adapted. Well done. Good job. I'm so fucking proud of you.

If I could see in this darkness, I would see you lying there, breathing, as you draw from your brain the camera-lens fictions you call your memories. You have been such a complete and utter fraud, haven't you, with all your lies to others and to yourself? Especially lying to yourself – to your *self*. You fucking idiot, lying to yourself, of all the asinine things you have done in your life, this has to be the ultimate in ignorance. You can't even separate the fact from the fiction, can you? This is exactly where you belong, stuck in the pitch for all eternity.

If we are truly the sum of our experiences, and those experiences are our memories, then *you – he – I... we* are nothing but a fiction. *You-he-I* do not really exist. We have warped our perception of ourselves so deeply there is no way for us to ever go back. How could we ever look at ourselves in the mirror, knowing what we know? How truly disconnected we have become, and it's purely self-inflicted. We are nobody. We are less than nobody. We have become the hypocrisy we so despise. No. We have not *become* hypocrites; we have always *been* hypocrites. Hell isn't other people; it's you.

Calm down, you shit! You're hyperventilating, and what's with the tears rolling down your cheeks? I thought you said you were never going to cry again. Wipe those fuckin' tears off your face. Suck it up. Isn't that what you tell people? "It's just life. Suck it up."

Wait. What's that noise? It's coming from the drain.

70

He gets control of his breathing so he can listen. He hears something. It's a familiar sound. Dripping, one after another. Drip... drip... drip. But it's not a drip. It's heavier, thicker. A splat. A plop.

You crawl over to the drain and put your ear over the hole. It is definitely coming from below and the sound is getting closer, rising in the pipe. The flow increases to a stream, rising faster towards you. It's bubbling up.

He reaches his hand down the conduit. He doesn't have to reach far. His fingers make contact. It's thick and warm, bubbling up to the surface. It overflows the drain and oozes onto the floor.

I stand. My feet are covered in it. I move to the door to get away but it's spreading out in all directions. It's now covering the floor and it's rising, quickly.

It's up to my ankles. What the fuck? It smells like oil but it's thicker and it's sticking to my feet so that I can hardly lift them. Shit.

He's at the door and he's pounding on it.

"Hey! Let me out! What's happening? What is this shit?

What are you doing to me? LET ME OUT!"

It's up to your knees and it won't stop rising. You trudge your way back to the centre of your cell. The liquid is becoming warmer and as you reach the middle, you feel the current of the flow on your feet as it streams up out of the drain.

The fluid rises up to his waist. He puts his fingers through the rebar and tries to lift himself above it. He can't. It's too thick, weighing him down. The smell, the consistency, the heat: it's tar. The cell is filling up with tar! It's getting hotter, burning your skin.

You scream. Your heart races. You can't think. Your face is pressed to the rebar.

I can't breath. The air's too thick. It's going to kill me. I'm going to drown in it.

It reaches his armpits, his chest, his shoulder blades. He is arched back, his lips and nose pressed to the metal. He is burning.

Suddenly, from above, blinding light, coming from the ventilation shaft, too bright after months of darkness.

He squeezes his eyes shut and tries to shield them with his arm.

It's no use. It's burning my eyes. I can't see. I can't breathe.

The tar swallows your ears and is creeping up, searing your face. It's over your eyes. You are being swallowed alive!

I am going to die alone!

He sucks in one last breath before being consumed by the pitch. Everything goes white.

71

They gather outside room B314 in the ICU, a rag-tag group of first-year residents beginning their rotation in Neurology. They are tired and overwhelmed but ready to take on new challenges.

A third year resident leads them through the process of "grand rounds".

"The patient was admitted to ER on Thursday evening. He was discovered unconscious by the river, appearing to have experienced a cycling accident that left him partially submerged in the cold water. It is estimated he had been in the water for fifteen to twenty minutes before being discovered. Emergency services assessed his vitals on scene. With an elevated heart rate and blood pressure, they treated him for hypothermia en route."

"There were no obvious injuries at the time, save for the expected cuts and contusions associated with falling, and rolling down a thirty foot embankment to the water. The patient was wearing a helmet and was assessed for head trauma. Manual inspection revealed nothing, but pupils were unresponsive."

"Blood work showed elevated red blood cells so a test of the cerebrospinal fluid was ordered. Combining these results with those from the CT and MRI, revealed a ruptured aneurysm in the occipital lobe, and he was taken to surgery."

"During surgery the patient began to exhibit signs of anaphylaxis, though there was no history of previous reactions in his medical records."

One of the residents inquires, "And the cause of the reaction?"

"No definitive cause. A small percentage of patients may react negatively to courses of IV medication. The reaction is not to the medications themselves, but the suspension medium. We changed out the tube and went with a different protocol to administer blood thinner and anti-inflammatories. A standard one-milligram dose of epinephrine was administered and the symptoms resolved."

"The procedure to repair the rupture went smoothly, but there was moderate swelling of the occipital and cerebellum extending to the spinal cord."

"In recovery the patient experienced a generalized tonic-clonic seizure. Seizures are always a possibility when there is swelling around the spinal cord. The patient was placed in soft restraint and treated with clonazepam."

"The seizure caused tachycardia resulting in v-fib. CPR was initiated and the patient was defibrillated three times before returning to normal sinus rhythm."

"He was transferred from Recovery to ICU last night and has experienced no further complications. We are just waiting for the swelling to subside and for the patient to regain consciousness. All of his vitals are stable and normal."

"Any questions?"

There are none.

"Then let's go in."

The patient is lying propped up in bed. He is no longer in restraints, but is still hooked up to an IV drip, and to heart and pulse monitors. His wife sits in a chair beside him.

The third year resident greets her and explains the presence of the other residents.

"Mind if we give him the once over?"

It was fine with her.

He pulls back the sheet covering the patient's feet and uses the dull end of a pen to check the plantar reflex. The patient's toes respond with a standard downward hallux flection.

"When he first came in," the third-year explains to the others, "he presented with a Babinski response, leading us to order the scans."

He stands beside the patient with a small flashlight in hand. He opens the lid of the right eye and checks for pupil response. It is normal. He opens the lid of the other and as he shines the light into the eye, the patient is suddenly awake, screaming, "I AM GOING TO DIE ALONE!"

72

He is in full panic, grasping at the side rails of the bed, trying to hold on, to resist whatever traumatic event he believes he is experiencing. He is suddenly covered in sweat, and beginning to hyperventilate.

The doctor sends the residents away and holds him down, calming him. "Please relax. Everything is fine. You are not going to die."

"Where am I?" he stammers, trying to catch his breath. "How did you find me?"

"You have been admitted to the Health Sciences Centre. A jogger found you in the park on Oak Street by the river. You need to settle down. Take deep breaths and try to relax."

His wife is now by his side, holding his hand. "Hon, you're going to be OK. You had to have emergency surgery but everything went just fine. We were all so worried about you."

"Did they send a rescue team? How did you get me out? Oh, thank you - you were able to get me out."

His wife looks confused. "Rescue team? Paramedics were called and they got you to the emergency department. Yes, they got you out of the water."

"Not water. Tar," he exclaims. "Burning tar. How did you find where they were holding me?"

The doctor steps in. "Sir, no one was holding you. You experienced a brain aneurysm while riding your bike. You lost consciousness and fell down an embankment into the river."

"No. That's wrong. They took me. They must have hit me over the head. I've been held in a dark cell for months." He is trying to make sense of everything.

"Hon, you need to settle down," his wife says, patting the back of his hand. "This happened on Thursday evening. It's now Sunday morning. You've been unconscious for three days, not months."

"No. It's not possible. It's - It's been months." He reaches up to feel his face. It is clean-shaven. "I had a beard and I haven't had a proper meal in..." He looks down at his protruding stomach. "...months."

"You're just a little confused, Honey. After what you've been through, it's not surprising."

"Sir, you've had a rough few days. Right now you just need to rest."

"But I swear," he insists, "I've been... They held me prisoner... I remember..."

"Patients under anesthetic can experience intense fugue-like hallucinations, especially in cases where there has been some injury to the brain. Your aneurysm was in the occipital region. It controls and interprets vision. You've probably been experiencing this phenomenon but, I assure you, you've only been here three days. Now, just lie back and get some rest. Would you like me to get you something to drink?"

"Please."

"I'll have someone bring you something." He leaves the room and heads for the nurses' station down the hall.

"I'm just so glad you're going to be OK," his wife says as she puts her arms around him gently and hugs him. He tentatively hugs her back.

"The girls are in a waiting area down the hall. I'm going to go let them know you're awake. I'll be right back," and she kisses him on the forehead before heading out the door.

He is alone in the room. He looks around, taking in his surroundings, the monitors and their beeping, the oxygen tank by the bed, the IV stuck in his hand.

"This can't be," he thinks. "It was real. The cell... all of it... all of that time I spent... thinking."

A nurse enters the room. He carries a tray with a large styrofoam container of water, a glass, and some packages of crackers. He's a muscular man in his late twenties or early thirties and he's sporting a shiner around the outside of his left eye.

"Here you go, a little water for you to drink. I brought you some crackers if you feel up to trying to eat. We'll start you off slow."

"Thank you."

"It's good to see you awake. It was touch and go there for a while yesterday."

"Yesterday?"

"You had a seizure after the operation and some other complications we had to take care of. I was your nurse in recovery."

"How'd you get the shiner?"

The nurse laughs as he touches the redness around his eye. "I was in the middle of checking your vitals when you seized. I'm afraid your elbow caught me before we had the chance to restrain your arms and legs."

"I'm sorry."

"No need to apologize, unless it was intentional," he

jokes. He puts the tray on a table and rolls it into place beside the bed. "Do you need some help with the water or the straw?"

"No. I should be fine."

"Well, just press the little button if you need anything. I'm just down the hall."

There is so much to process. "It wasn't real - just a hallucination from the anesthetic. Only three days." It is all so inconceivable.

He hears voices coming down the hall, his wife and daughters. She is trying to keep them quiet. They enter the room. The girls flock to his side, their voices overlapping with "Daddy." "I was so worried." "Are you gonna be OK?" "Can you come home?"

"He's going to be fine, girls. No, he can't come home for a while yet." She turns to her husband, "The doctor said they could come and see you but we should keep it short."

The girls take turns hugging their father and telling him all sorts of things about the last few days. He is getting overwhelmed and his wife sees it in his eyes.

"OK, ladies. That's enough for now. I'll take you back down to the waiting area. Maybe we can go grab some lunch and let Dad rest."

He nods to let her know it's a good idea.

Before she leaves, she says, "There's someone else who'd like to see you if you feel up to it."

"Who?"

"Are you up to it?"

"Sure."

"I'll send him down."

A few minutes later Junior walks in. "How you doin', Bro?"

"What are you doing here?"

"Nice to see you, too."

"No. I meant..."

"It's OK. You must be on the mend."

"Sorry, I... Thank you for coming."

"Sport gave me a call to let me know what was goin' on. Of course I came to see you. You're my brother, the only family I've got."

"Well... thanks."

"No problem."

Junior pulls up a chair and takes a seat. "Why don't you try to get some sleep? I'll just sit here 'til they get back."

For the next hour, his brother watches him sleep.

Two days later I am up and walking around. The IV has been removed and I no longer need all the monitor wires. I've been moved to a regular room and I'm actually enjoying eating the meals the hospital provides.

I sit in a chair by the window looking out at the view from the sixth floor, still trying to wrap my head around everything that has actually happened versus everything I *believed* had happened. It will take time to sort the fact from the fiction.

By the end of the week, the bandages are removed. My hair has been shaved off. There is a small scar on the back of my skull. "Not like there was much hair back there to begin with. I should grow it back, though, to cover things up."

One final series of tests and the doctors release me from the hospital. My wife picks me up and drives me home.

It has only been two weeks, but for me, it still feels like months.

We approach the house and pull into the attached garage. The automatic door closes behind us. My bike is leaning up against the wall, having been returned. The front wheel looks like some twisted, hideous piece of contemporary sculpture. "I'll have to get that fixed."

I enter my home. Nothing has really changed.

"Would you like me to make you something to eat?" my wife asks.

"No, thanks. I'm a bit tired. I think I'll just head upstairs and lie down for a bit."

I climb the stairs and peek into the girls' rooms. They're all still at school. "Messy as always."

At the end of the hall I enter the bedroom. Everything is the same as I left it. It just seems so odd. I have yet to come to terms with time.

My wife has placed my satchel beside the bed, recovered the evening of my – incident. It managed to not land in the water.

I take my cellphone from the bag. It's out of juice, so I pull out the charger and plug it into the outlet by the window. Once it is charged enough to turn on, I check to see if I have any phone messages. There are a few, mostly people from work calling to say they are happy to hear that I'm feeling better.

The last message is from the author who is now on the Board at the college.

"Oh, hello. Just returning your call from last Thursday. Yes, I do remember you from the launch of my latest book. Smyth really does know how to put on quite the show. As to your inquiry regarding my assistance with your, um, situation with the dean, well, I'm not sure there's all that much I can do, really. My position with the Board is an honourary one. The college gave me the position as a bit of a PR stunt, actually. I don't really know any of the other Board members all that well and I've only met the dean of your department over drinks at a faculty dinner..."

I delete the message and place the phone on the windowsill to finish charging.

"What the hell was I thinking, calling her?"

I sit on the end of the bed and find myself looking at my reflection in the hinged, tri-panel mirror above the chest of drawers. Three slightly different perspectives of me look back.

I examine my face. It's tired and worn. "Maybe I'll grow the beard back." I catch himself mid-thought. "You've never had a beard," I say aloud to the mirror.

I can't change what I know, what I've learned… revealed. I can't erase the experience. It's not possible. Real or not, it was an experience, none the less.

So what now?

"You have some choices to make, don't you?" I whisper to my reflections.

My eyes lose focus to the empty space in between. "Yes. Yes *we* do."

"Time present and time past
Are both perhaps present in our time future,
And time future contained in time past.
If all time is eternally present
All time is unredeemable.
What might have been is an abstraction
Remaining a perpetual possibility
Only in a world of speculation.
What might have been and what has been
Point to one end, which is always present.
Footfalls echo in the memory
Down the passage which we did not take
Towards the door we never opened
Into the rose-garden. My words echo
Thus, in your mind."
— T.S. Eliot

Out of the Pitch

NOTES

As I get older, I find myself looking back at a life lived. In those reflections, I have discovered inconsistencies, gaps and altered visions. Through my own personal remembrances, the idea for this novel took shape. If we are the sum of our memories, our stories, then who are we when those reflections have been altered over time?

I offer my gratitude to my beta readers: Deighton Thomas, Lily Keightley, Sookie Mei, Steve Thomas, and Susan Marshall. Their input nudged me in new directions that I hadn't even considered when writing the first draft.

My thanks, especially, to Kenna Marshall, my mother-in-law and my editor. She is thorough and blunt and her suggestions have helped to sculpt this story and its telling.

A fellow independent author, Robert Chazz Chute, wrote three novels in "The Hitman Series". He made an interesting choice and wrote them in second person. I was fascinated by the voice and wanted to play with it. That simple fact became a major inspiration for the shape of this novel, so I'd like to thank him for taking the risk.

Gratitude to RW, who guided my imagination.

For setting me on a better path, my thanks to the three witches.

Please check out my first novel, INTERSECTION, available through CreateSpace and Amazon. You will also find CDs of my original music, HARBINGER, and CALM BEFORE THE STORM and my poetry anthology, AT ONE – A LIFE'S SENTENCE.

Visit and "like" my singer/songwriter page on Facebook stop by www.reverbnation.com/davesemple for some music.

Keep up to date at Harbinger Press/Media of Facebook.

INTERSECTION

What people have said about Dave's first novel, INTERSECTION.

"You gotta read it… it's important." - Deighton Thomas

"Dave Semple already writes like a seasoned author. His characters, dialog, and narration are well written. The story flows at a good pace and the climax of the story is definitely worthy of the journey through the lives of the characters, leaving the reader with a desire to go back and re-read some of the chapters after reaching the end. I recommend this book as something that should have general appeal to a grown up audience wanting to enjoy a good story." - Paul Battersby

"OK, when's the next one! I can't tell you how much I enjoyed it!" - Sheila Paterson

"I could not put it down. It was so well written and easy to read I did not want it to end." - April Chappell

"Excellent read. Great sense of place. Wonderful characters and a splendid twist. (Semple is) a keen observer of human nature and has an authentic understanding of the complexities of human relationships. A wonderful read! Can't wait for the next one." - John Turner

"A week after finishing the book, I found myself missing the characters and wondering what they were up to." – Claire Porter-Martin

Dave Semple

Made in the USA
Columbia, SC
21 October 2017